PLANNING
the
IMPOSSIBLE

PLANNING THE

Impossible

by Mavis Jukes

A Yearling Book

Published by
Dell Yearling
an imprint of
Random House Children's Books
a division of Random House, Inc.
1540 Broadway
New York, New York 10036

Visit us on the Web! www.randomhouse.com/kids

Educators and librarians, for a variety of teaching tools, visit us at www.randomhouse.com/teachers

ISBN: 0-440-41230-7

Reprinted by arrangement with Delacorte Press

Printed in the United States of America

December 2000

10 9 8 7 6 5 4 3 2 1

OPM

For Sonia and Dixon

One

"**WHO'S CLASS COURIER?**" Mr. Elmo mumbled. He looked at the job list written on the board.

This is ridiculous, thought River. "I am," she told him.

Mr. Elmo held up a stack of flyers. "I would like you to make sure every upper-grade teacher has one of these to post before the end of the day. And please give Mrs. Bagley one for the office bulletin board."

"Okay," said River.

He put the stack on his desk. "Alrighty, then." He helped himself to the one on top and carefully hung it from a clip above the board. FOURTH ANNUAL POWWOW AT THE PARK was written above a photo of a Native American man in spectacular dance regalia.

"For those of you who are interested in beefing up your social studies grade," said Mr. Elmo, looking straight at

Henry, "you can get twenty culture points for attending the powwow. It's this Saturday, in Live Oak Park."

Beefing up? What a distasteful expression—especially for a vegetarian, which River sometimes was. Unless an Indian taco got within snapping distance.

River didn't need to beef any grades up; she was a straight-A student. But she'd gone to every last powwow with her mom, dad and older sister, Megan. She even knew one of the Pomo dancers; they'd gone to preschool together.

Yup. River would be going to the powwow again this year. And scarfin' down an Indian taco. Mmmmm-mmmm. Spiced ground beef and garlic, refried beans, diced tomatoes, lettuce, grated cheese and hot sauce—and onions—on fry bread. Wait a minute! The powwow was *this* weekend? Well, *that* sucks, she told herself.

River not only had to miss the All-Stars baseball practice on Friday after school—now she'd also have to miss the powwow. All because Aunt Colleen was coming to San Francisco from Chicago! Darn it anyway!

"Uh—Mr. Elmo?" said Kirstin. "*My* guidebook group can't go to that powwow thing." She paused. "We'll all be chillin' at our *limo party* this Saturday."

Like anybody cares, thought River.

"And there's *no way* we're rescheduling," said Kirstin. "We're totally psyched about finishing the party guide. The only thing we can't really figure out is, like, whether to call our guidebook *Guide to a Sweet Ride* or *How to Have a Limo Blast*." She surveyed the class with a self-satisfied expression.

"Kirstin?" said Mr. Elmo. "Why shouldn't having a

2

limo shindig include attending a powwow for an hour? Any limo driver worth his salt will know his way to Live Oak Park."

"Mr. Elmo?" said a small voice.

"E-e-e-e-yes, Margaret?"

"I have a complaint."

"Well, hang on, Margaret. I haven't even got the schedule up and you're already griping." Mr. Elmo turned his back and began writing the day's schedule on the board. A little tuft of gray hair was poking out of the hole in the back of his Orioles cap, between the plastic strap and the fabric.

Frightful!

River opened up the clasp envelope that held the first draft of her group's *Guidebook for Sixth-Grade Parents*. She located the sheet of paper that said *Unacceptable Expressions for Adults to Use in the Presence of Preadolescents* and wrote *alrighty, then, beefing up, worth his salt* and *shindig* at the bottom of the list.

Then she quickly flipped to the first draft of the rules section of the guidebook and, in the margin, jotted down *No hair poking out of hats.* She nibbled on her bottom lip for a minute and added *No allowing hat to squash down hair and make it stick to head. Once on, leave hat on.*

This rule pertained to River's father, who actually had hair.

Not Elmo. Who had fringe. She glanced up at the schedule Mr. Elmo was writing. So far, so good—except that it was a Furley morning.

During most of the sixth grade, three mornings a week, for one hour per morning, all sixth-graders at Franklin School who had turned in parent permission slips were subjected to the cheerful yapping of Mrs. Gladys B. Furley, R.N.

Mrs. Furley had already taught the students more information than any of them wanted to know about Human Interaction, a.k.a. Sex Ed. And now that the year was almost over, Furley was turning up the heat: The woman was showing up as many as four times a week, to review. As if the information weren't bad enough the first time through!

"Okle dokle," said Mr. Elmo. "Any questions about today's activities?"

"We need more time for guidebooks," said Jules.

River added *okle dokle* to the Unacceptable Expressions list.

"But I'm always getting squeezed by your group for more guidebook time," said Mr. Elmo. "Use time wisely, Jules; plan, plan, plan—don't always expect extensions. Meet deadlines; you're practically in junior high!"

River added *plan, plan, plan* and *wisely* to the list.

"Yeah," said Kirstin. " 'Cause, like, no offense, Jules, but your guidebook group should get organized. The limo group's *megaorganized*. We don't need more time. Why should you?"

The class grew very quiet.

"Twenty more minutes, then," said Mr. Elmo suddenly. "If you really think it's necessary, Jules." He began revising the schedule on the board.

River smiled to herself. One point for Jules, and none for Kirstin. Or: one point for Jules's group, which included River, and a big fat zero for the limo group.

Ha! This was turning out to be quite a good day already.

Just think: twenty extra minutes of working with—mmmmm! mmmmm!—DB. And the rest of the kids in the guidebook group: Jules, the leader; Henry, who liked Jules; Margaret, River's childhood friend; and Noah, Margaret's boyfriend.

River only regretted that her best friend, Candace, hadn't yet returned from her trip to Hawaii. Candace would have been able to provide invaluable insight for a guidebook for sixth-grade parents. Not only had she been able to expand the Take Our Daughters to Work Day concept into an extended outing at a landscaping conference on the island of Oahu, but she had done such an excellent job of modifying her parents' behavior that they could be taken anywhere.

Even to a luau on the beach!

But even without Candace, River loved guidebook time. And the *Guidebook for Sixth-Grade Parents* was coming along very nicely, if she did say so herself. Each and every student in her group had made at least one valuable contribution. Except Margaret, who was still too immature to understand why a Parent Behavior Modification Plan needed to be put in place.

River admired their long list of carefully drafted rules.

What a masterful document! There should be one on every bookshelf. And maybe there would be. According to Mr. Elmo's plan, each parent, student, friend or family member who came to Franklin School to attend the Sixth-Grade Farewell Event would be given a hundred Book Bucks and a chance to spend them on guidebooks, how-to books or other informational materials that Mr. Elmo's students had written, edited, designed, illustrated and published.

River's group was bound to sell every last copy—if not to the parents of sixth-graders, then to the sixth-grade students themselves.

The *Guidebook for Sixth-Grade Parents* would be accompanied by a separate booklet of blank citation forms that could be filled out by kids and issued to parents who did not—*or would not*—comply with the regulations.

"Mr. Elmo?" said Margaret. "Can we go back to something for a minute? Why did you say *his* salt? Who's to say their limo driver's going to be a *guy*? Women can't drive?"

"Ah," said Mr. Elmo. "My feminist activist: Mizzz Rothrock. Ya caught me." He turned to the board and credited the class with a good behavior point, as a penalty to himself.

Kirstin looked over at Margaret. "Our limo driver is totally going to be a *guy*. It's a guy in a tux. You think we'd toss forty bucks an hour for a *woman* to drive us? What would she *wear*?"

Margaret turned to Noah and whispered, "It's official: Kirstin's a moron."

"You're, like, *totally out of it*, Margaret!" cried Kirstin.

"Oohhhh," whispered Margaret to Noah. "So I'm first on her dis list—like I care?"

"Kirstin?" said Mr. Elmo. "I'm warning you."

"Warning *me*?" said Kirstin. "Margaret's the one who, like, started it!"

"Oh yes, Kirstin," Mr. Elmo muttered with a sigh. "It's always somebody else, isn't it?" He set the erasable marker on the tray below the board. He opened his desk drawer and took out a roll of masking tape. "Anyway, I thought you guys *had* that limo party already," he said quietly as he reinforced the repair on his glasses frames.

Kirstin stared at him with a look of mock disbelief. "Uh—Mr. Elmo?"

"Yes?"

"Hel-lo! This is, like, our *third* limo party?"

"Is that a question? Or a statement? And Kirstin?" said Mr. Elmo.

"Eeeeyeah?" said Kirstin after a long blink.

"Why are you looking at me as though I'm stupid?"

Mr. Elmo put on his glasses. He seated the frames in a good position on the bridge of his nose. Then he raised and lowered his eyebrows a few times to test the comfort level. There was a snarled-up hair trapped in the tape.

Get thee to Lenscrafters! River commanded him, to herself.

"Uh—it's just . . . like, how would my group be savvy enough to write the ultimate limo party guidebook?" said Kirstin. "If we only had one party?"

"Her and I each had limo birthday parties," Stella broke in, in a patronizing voice.

"*She* and I, Stella. Not *her* and I. Learn grammar," said Mr. Elmo. "You're practically in the seventh grade."

"Oh," whispered Kirstin. "Pardough-nay us." She rested her burgundy fingertips on the front of her blouse.

"*Anyway,*" continued Stella. "She and me, we told our moms we had to test things out, kind of research stuff—for your assignment, in case there were probs to solve."

"She and me?" said Mr. Elmo.

"*What*ever," said Stella with a grand roll of her eyeballs. "Anyway, our parents totally bought it," she said

7

with a giggle. "And . . ." She glanced around the room, catching the eyes of the limo invitees. "I have some excellent news! Here's the lowdown: I talked my mom into buying everyone a disposable camera for a party favor—so we can, like, document stuff!" A couple of the partygoers gasped with delight. "Plus, we can totally get great shots of the snacks!"

"Our moms are making all the snacks," Kirstin explained, assuming somebody cared—which River certainly didn't.

"Your *dads* can't cook?" Margaret asked her.

Kirstin ignored her. She flipped her hair from one side to the other. "We are so *psyched* to find the perfect recipes! *I'm* in charge of the snack section." She put her hand on her chest to emphasize the *I'm*. "And the snack section is gonna *rock*."

River looked at the front of Kirstin's blouse. GUESS? was written in script on the pocket. Guess what? Guess how Kirstin's bra size seemed to have quadrupled overnight?

Mr. Elmo took off his glasses and squeezed and molded the tape. "Powwow. Ten till seven. To get credited for culture points, it is required that you present a ticket stub to me on Monday. The cost of admission is three dollars; kids twelve and under, free."

"How do we get a ticket stub?" asked Henry. "If we're under twelve and don't need a ticket to get in?"

"Life is full of challenges, Henry," said Mr. Elmo. "And you, my friend, are one of my great, great challenges." He smiled affectionately at Henry. Then, for reasons known only to himself, Mr. Elmo turned his baseball cap sideways, so that the brim shaded his ear. "You figure it out. The Grand Entry begins at one. Be there or be square."

Yikes! Now some fringe from the *side* of Mr. Elmo's head was poking out of the hole in the back of the hat!

"On the subject of cameras, remember—do *not* take a photo of a Native American in dance regalia without asking," Mr. Elmo told the class.

~~Kirstin dropped her mouth open. She made~~ a little Uh! noise. "Well, like, who took the picture on the flyer then?"

"Someone who asked permission first," said Mr. Elmo calmly.

"Oh, puh-leeze," said Stella.

Mr. Elmo turned and looked at her. "What do you mean, 'Oh, please'?"

"What do I *mean*? What I mean is—Indians should be totally pumped that people like us want to click some pix of them."

"Nonsense," said Mr. Elmo. "And what do you mean, 'people like *us*'?"

Stella said nothing.

"Respect, Stella. That's what culture points are all about."

Stella smirked.

"And what's funny?"

"Nothing." Stella folded her arms on her chest and looked over at Kirstin.

"Hello, Frank!" said a cheery voice from the doorway. Mrs. Furley had arrived. "I like the hat!" she told him. "You look like a r-r-rappa!"

River winced. She wrote *Be there or be square* and *rappa* at the bottom of the Unacceptable Expressions list.

Mr. Elmo stood at attention, knocking the heels of his stadium boots together with a thud. He snapped a salute off the brim of the cap. Then he picked up his briefcase and headed out the door.

What a fast exit, thought River.

It must be Donut Day in the faculty room.

Two

MRS. FURLEY LOOKED around the room. "Ah," she said, nodding at the flyer. "The powwow. I missed it the past couple of years, but I'm hoping to go on Saturday. I love those Apache shawls! I wish I had one!"

She put her arms out like wings and turned a couple of times while doing some fancy footwork.

Help! cried River to herself. Didn't the woman know that *all dancing*—including Apache-type dancing—was against the rules for grownies?

Mrs. Furley slid out of her cardigan sweater and hung it on the back of Mr. Elmo's chair. "Anyway"—her face lit up—"good morning, all of you brilliant people! Everybody ready for Bird and Bee Hour?"

With a sigh, River lifted her desktop and took out her Human Interaction notebook.

Mrs. Furley made a buzzing sound and flapped her

elbows a few times as she roamed around the room, placing a sheet of paper on every student's desk. "I think you're going to find our very last assignment the most interesting one of all!"

Henry groaned and she ignored him.

"In fact, that's why I saved it for last," she said.

River looked down at the assignment sheet. The method of reproduction of . . . *a mushroom?*

Gosh, River thought. What a pain.

The end of the year was in sight; everything was winding down. Why another report? The sixth-graders were practically seventh-graders. Why couldn't Furley give Sex Ed a rest? It was May already!

River gazed out the window.

Nobody was interested in the courtship of mushrooms. They'd been fertilized or else they hadn't, and nobody cared either way. The bushes in the courtyard had bloomed and mated and dropped their petals. The sun was high and hot . . .

River suddenly sat straight up. *Deodorant!* Had she remembered deodorant? She tipped her head to one side and pretended to itch her cheek against her shoulder and gave her pit a subtle sniff.

She could smell the light springish scent of her big sister's Bouquet of Spring Light Scent antiperspirant. Good.

"So," continued Mrs. Furley, "you will each choose a living organism . . . including any kind of plant from a tree to a mushroom, any animal big or small, or anything else that's alive, including bacteria and viruses. And molds. And do a brief written report on the organism's

12

method of reproduction. Be prepared to discuss its court-ship process, if it has any."

Mrs. Furley leaned against Mr. Elmo's desk. She looked off into space for a moment, gathering her thoughts.

Sunlight was coming into the classroom from the left and it lit the side of Mrs. Furley's face and hair. To River, she looked a little like a Rembrandt portrait; there was even a little golden light in her eyebrows.

Hmmmm. If Gladys Furley lost the two barrettes and got different glasses frames, she really would be a very attractive woman. For an older person.

How old was she—forty?

And she had a pretty good body, too: good arms, except for when she reached up to write on the board in a sleeveless shirt and the underneath part got to jiggling in a scary way.

Yes. Gladys Furley was very attractive, as long as she stuck with sleeves. And River didn't blame Margaret for thinking that maybe, just maybe, Mrs. Furley could be hooked up with Margaret's dad. So Margaret could have Mrs. Furley for a stepmom. Margaret needed a stepmom! So Margaret could stop asking River so many embarrass-ing questions!

"River?"

River jumped. "Yes?"

"Do me a favor, would you?" said Mrs. Furley. "Close just that one blind for me."

"I'll do it," said Henry. He reached over and lowered the blind until the sunlight disappeared from Mrs. Furley's face.

"Good enough. Thank you—leave it like that."

How annoying! The blind was tipped. Why would Henry leave a blind partway down and tipped on a slant?

It was like the throw rug that River's dad left rumpled on the bathroom floor. Or the towels he left stuffed behind the towel bar, without evening up the ends . . .

"Why are you frowning?" Mrs. Furley asked River.

"Why is she *frowning*?" said Margaret. "Look at the way Henry left the blind!" She marched over and fixed it.

River smiled to herself. There were advantages in having lifelong friends, especially if one of them happened to be Margaret Rothrock. They'd been together since preschool.

Sweet little tough little Margaret.

Ya had to love her!

River heard someone whisper, "Sit down, you little neat geek." And she saw Margaret whip her head around and look at Kirstin.

Kirstin and Margaret stared at each other for a moment.

Kirstin mouthed the words, "You're a freak!" and somebody giggled.

"Ba-a-a-a-a-a!" said Margaret suddenly.

"Girls?" said Mrs. Furley. "That's enough."

"You're a sheep!" Margaret said in a loud voice, and the class grew very quiet.

"I said," said Mrs. Furley, "that's enough." Her eyes followed Margaret as Margaret returned to her seat.

Would Mrs. Furley love having Margaret for a stepdaughter?

Of course she would!

Here was Furley: divorced, and with no children around to keep her from carrying on in the public schools about periods and premenstrual syndrome.

And then there was Margaret: a motherless child, desperately in need of a mom-type woman to take her shopping for things like maybe the world's tiniest training bra.

And then we had Margaret's dad, Jim: a handsome ~~widower who would probably love nothing~~ better than to stay home from the mall while his daughter and new wife, Gladys, snooped through the Macy's lingerie department with their arms slung around each other—without the slightest concern about guidebook rule violations.

Mrs. Furley lowered her voice to a whisper. "The courtship process!" she said dramatically. "The fascinating, intriguing courtship shenanigans of the critters on Planet Earth . . . courtship behaviors. They amaze me!" She glanced at the faces of the students. "Do you know a luna moth can draw a mate to her by squeaking her leg hairs together—draw a mate from far, far away?"

Shaving gel!

That was it!

River *knew* she'd forgotten to add something to the shopping list at home!

"Anyway, topics are due next class meeting," Mrs. Furley was telling the class. She made herself comfortable by sitting on the edge of Mr. Elmo's desk. She stretched out her legs and crossed one shoe over the other. "Today we'll continue to review puberty in males and the male reproductive gear," she announced. "Then on we'll go—to our final review of the specifics of reproduction. Okay?

"Henry?" said Mrs. Furley. "Would you bring me that *Teacher's Guide to Human Interaction*?" She pointed to a fat book on the counter beside his desk. "I'd like to review that short section about reproduction in general—to get you puzzling about topics for your reports."

Henry carefully picked up the guide as if it had germs and brought it to Mrs. Furley.

"If hearing this passage again doesn't spark an idea," she told the class, "be sure to check out the listings for nature programs on PBS. Some of these independent filmmakers document the most marvelous animal courtship behaviors!" She pushed her glasses farther up the bridge of her nose and began browsing through the teacher's guide.

"Mrs. Furley?"

"What, Margaret?"

"Did you know that in New Zealand it's culturally inappropriate to prop your rear end up on a table or desktop, or to sit on a table or desktop?"

"No, I didn't, Margaret. But I'll keep that in mind if I ever get pooped in New Zealand. What page do I want?" Mrs. Furley mumbled.

"Why don't you use a bookmark?" Noah asked her.

"Good suggestion, Noah," said Mrs. Furley quietly. "I'll take it into consideration. Along with where I should and shouldn't park my rump when traveling in foreign territory. Ah! 'Chapter Seven,' " she read in a strong voice. " 'Sex and Pregnancy. The Birds and the Bees.' "

"Mrs. Furley?" said Margaret.

"Now what?"

"My dad has spare bookmarks at home and I'll bring you one."

"Good," said Mrs. Furley.

"With his business's name on them," said Margaret. "And his office telephone number and the address."

"Ah."

"And his office e-mail address."

"Thank you, Margaret," said Mrs. Furley. She began to read:

> *"To reproduce means to make anew; to make again. All living creatures reproduce, from the tiniest moth to the largest rhinoceros—and some of them reproduce . . . sexually. No species could continue to inhabit the earth without having the ability to reproduce."*

Margaret's eyes widened. She turned to River. "Bees have sex?" she whispered.

River shrugged.

> *"When creatures reproduce sexually, it means the male and female parents each contribute genes to their offspring. Genes carry the information needed to form new life—"*

"River!" whispered Margaret. "Do birds?"

"Shhh!" said River.

"Ahem," said Mrs. Furley. She looked up from her book in Margaret's direction. "May I go on?

> *"Genes are contained in the female's egg and in the reproductive cells of the male and are united during the mating process.*

*"Not all living things reproduce sexually, so
not all living things have sex organs. Here are
some that do: flowering plants, insects, reptiles,
amphibians, fish, birds, and mammals—"*

Margaret heaved an enormous sigh. "Mrs. Furley?"
she said. "Now *come on.*"

" 'Come on' what, Margaret?"

"You're not *actually* going to try to tell us that bees
have—" Margaret cleared her throat and stared at Mrs.
Furley for a long moment.

"Have what, Margaret? We need to get used to using
correct terminology. A clearing of the throat does not
equal a word. Are you asking me about bee reproductive
organs? Is that your question?"

River made a face. What was the matter with the
woman?

"If it is, the answer is: They must," said Mrs. Furley.
"And I'd like to know more about 'em, wouldn't you?"

Margaret shrugged. "I suppose so. But I don't know
for what purpose I would use the information."

"It's useful just to know stuff, Margles. We've talked
about this before. Didn't you tell me you want to grow up
to be an expert? Like Dr. Ruth?"

"Maybe—but I didn't expect you to headline it."

"Sorry. But *do* pick the bee for your final report. 'The
Reproductive Activity of Bees'! You become our resident
bee expert. Get up and on the computer right now, if you
want."

"It's been down for three weeks," said Noah. He and
Margaret exchanged an exasperated look.

"Can't Margaret use the computers in the library?" asked Mrs. Furley.

"I suppose," said Noah.

"Go to the library at lunch, then," Mrs. Furley told Margaret. "And get on that Internet. Find out about royal jelly—"

"I can't because Mrs. Fitch won't tell me the secret code," said Margaret.

"Well, have you signed pledge papers?"

"No."

"Then sign them."

"I can't sign pledge papers because my dad doesn't want me on the Internet at school. My cousin Helen told him kids can get access to inappropriate information—"

"Which is why we have the pledge system," interrupted Mrs. Furley.

"So," continued Margaret, "if *you* expect *me* to do research on the Internet, *you're* going to have to talk to *my dad* about it." She quickly scribbled something on a small piece of paper and held it out. "Here's his unlisted home phone number—and pager number."

"Thank you, Margaret," said Mrs. Furley, approaching the end of her patience. She took the paper from Margaret and folded it in half, then tucked it into her breast pocket.

"You'll lose it there!" cried Margaret. "Don't you have a Rolodex? Or an address book?"

Mrs. Furley took a deep breath and exhaled. She looked over the top of her glasses at Margaret for a long moment. "Margaret? I've got twenty-eight students in this class. Please. Don't monopolize the program."

"Sorry," said Margaret quietly. She looked down at the notebook on her desk.

"Yeah," whispered Kirstin, "so *shut up*, Little Miss Motor Mouth."

Mrs. Furley began again. "Think about it." She tried to look very, very thoughtful. "Last project of the year . . . Each and every one of you has an opportunity to investigate something which is truly intriguing to you. Think. Think. Think. All of the millions and millions of species of living things must reproduce . . . including us, of course."

With all this fascinating Furleytalk about reproduction, River couldn't help wondering:

How soon till lunch?

She checked her watch.

Time was standing still.

Mrs. Furley began to read out loud again. " 'Flowers have pretty lit-tle dus-ty sex organs,' " she continued in a happy voice. " 'Bees help flowering plants mate by carrying their pollen from blossom to blossom—' "

"That's nice of 'em!" said Noah. "To truck that stuff around."

Mrs. Furley turned the page. " 'Apples, oranges, pears, peaches and other fruits are the ripened ovaries of flowers.' " She looked up from her book to survey the reaction of the students.

"Henry?"

"Yes?"

"Pay attention."

"I am."

"You are not. If you were paying attention, you would

20

have made a wisecrack about what I just said about peaches and pears being ovaries."

"Oh."

"Wait!" said Margaret suddenly. "Don't call my dad tonight because he'll still be in El Paso, Texas. Where he just bought himself lizard-skin cowboy boots!"

"Fine."

~~"And Mrs. Furley? I don't want to~~ monopolize the program but I need to say one more thing: Even if my dad says yes—I want you to know that I don't really like to cruise the information highway. I'm more into the idea of community and communication."

"Well, what about a chat room?" said Mrs. Furley. "People communicate in chat rooms. Don't they?"

"Go to a chat room . . . to chat about bee sex?" said Margaret.

"Well . . ."

"*That's* considered appropriate for *school*?"

Mrs. Furley frowned. "I'd have to think about that, I guess."

"I *hate* researching on the Internet," said Margaret, getting more irritated by the minute. "I don't *care* about what Dr. Bee Boy from Yale writes in his thesis about royal jam."

River smiled to herself.

"Calm down," said Mrs. Furley. "*Please!* My instructions were: You can pick any kind of a living creature, big or small—fish or fowl—"

Margaret interrupted. "And as far as the PBS animal programs are concerned, I don't *care* what some nerd with a camera in a rubber diving suit claims she's observing about the dating habits of shrimp!"

Mrs. Furley raised her palms in the air. "How did we get onto shrimp?" she whispered to the ceiling.

"When I do reports, I like the interview format," continued Margaret, now on a roll. "I like the person-to-person approach. Interacting with real people! So I've been mulling over an idea for . . ." She paused. "A kind of survey."

Mrs. Furley let out a faint moan, from a high note down to a low note. "About what, Margaret?"

"About the pros and cons of having a certain . . . thing."

"What certain . . . thing?"

Margaret made aggressive eye contact with Mrs. Furley. "I'll *tell* you later."

"Okay. Tell me later. Anyone else in the class want to do an alternate report? You can. But be serious about it," said Mrs. Furley. "No nonsense. I mean it. I expect you to be completely appropriate and to use scientific terms at all times." She stared for a moment at Henry, the class clown.

"What!" said Henry.

She lifted an eyebrow at him. Then she looked down at the book again. "Where was I," she said. "Ah! 'Most species of animals can mate only with each other: bees with bees, birds with birds, goats with goats,' " she continued. She turned the page. " 'All of us who reproduce sexually have our own unique and mysterious ways of courting each other. These courtships result in the reproduction of our species.' "

Mrs. Furley shut her finger in the book to hold the

place and smiled at the class. " 'Our own unique and mysterious ways of courting each other.' Think about it. Ever seen a peacock open his spectacular fan of tail feathers to impress a peahen? Ever seen a robin poke out his red breast to attract a mate?"

Henry and DB looked sideways at each other. "Robin dudes have *boobs*?" whispered Henry. "Bummer!"

Three

RIVER SAT ON THE COUCH between Megan and her dad. Her mom was taking up the whole love seat, with her feet up on the ottoman. The middle two buttons of her maternity shirt had popped open, and she was gazing at her belly. "I used to be an innie and now I'm an outie," she announced.

"Mom?" said River. "Thank you for sharing. We've noticed."

"Stop nibbling your nails," said River's mom.

"Shhh," said River. "I'm supposed to watch this."

The Discovery Channel was on. A wild mountain goat with tall, sharp horns was galloping toward a boulder lying in the dirt. He knocked it with his horns and came to an abrupt stop. He gazed at the rock, then turned and trotted away. He stopped and pawed the ground with one hoof. In

24

the background, two or three other goats were watching him.

What was with this guy?

The goat reared up on his hind legs and came back down again. He lowered his head. Then he took another run at the rock. He bashed it and it tumbled over.

"Yes!" cried River's dad. He stood up and triumphantly lifted his fists in the air.

Megan turned to her father. "Dad?" she said.

"Sorry," said her father. He sat back down.

"Suddenly we understand why your father's a geologist," said River's mother. "It's an expression of the instinctive male attraction to rocks."

The goat lifted his noble head, and the camera zoomed in. The whiskers on his chin stirred in the breeze. He stuck the end of his tongue up one nostril. Then he extended his lips and loudly bleated, displaying a row of horrid yellow flat teeth.

The commentator, in her strong British accent, began carrying on about magnificent specimens. The camera cut to a female goat.

She flicked her tail.

River turned to her mother. "You know what?" she said. "I'm so sick of the Human Interaction sex review I'm thinking of asking for a job working in the school office during Furley time."

"She even threw her notes out," said Megan. "I saw her."

"Only one diagram," said River.

"Of what?" said River's mom.

River didn't answer.

"Guy stuff," said Megan.

"Ah—yes. Well. Let me tell you *my* take on males and puberty," said their mother. *"Grubbing, grooming, grunting.* These three little words say it all—"

"Mom?" said River.

"They eat, comb their hair, shave invisible mustaches, splash themselves with men's cologne—all the while limiting their vocabularies to one- or two-syllable grunts. Grubbing, grooming, ~~grunting: the three clues that let the~~ world know that puberty has hit the male."

River ignored her.

"And there's one more unmistakable clue: Suddenly, inexplicably, boys are able to eat chocolate ice cream without leaving an outline around the mouth."

Megan picked up the remote and pressed Mute. "Mom? Get a clue: Nobody wants to talk about this. But we do want to know something: What *is* the deal with this weekend again?"

"Yeah," said River grumpily, "that's what I've been wondering."

"It's simple," said their mom. "Aunt Colleen is flying into San Francisco airport early Friday morning to attend a seminar on software or something. On Friday afternoon, the four of us will toodle into the city and take her to dinner. After dinner, you two will bunk with Colleen in her suite. She's got two bedrooms and a sitting room." She caught her husband's eye. "And *your father and I* will have *our own separate room.*" She batted her eyelashes at him and he smiled.

Megan eyed them suspiciously.

"Saturday is Colleen's birthday," continued their mother. "We'll need to bring her a present—that can be your department. We'll spend the day seeing the sights, and then come back home at about five or so. Colleen will take off bright and early on Sunday morning to return to Chicago."

"I hope you know the powwow in the park is on Saturday," grumbled River.

"This Saturday? What a shame!" said River's mom. "That'll be the first time we miss it. But I did promise Colleen we'd have crab omelettes at Fisherman's Wharf. Then we'd ride the cable cars or take the ferry and—"

Megan groaned.

"And maybe go to the Exploratorium. You love the Exploratorium! It's totally a hoot!"

"We *hate* the Exploratorium!" said Megan. "Besides, Anton and I just figured out: Saturday is our nine-month anniversary. We want to hang out at the powwow together."

"You know what?" said their mother. "This highly irks me!"

Add it to the list! thought River. Along with *toodle* and *bunk with*.

"We agreed to this plan weeks ago!" complained their mother.

"But you *never* told us it was powwow weekend," said River. "I *need* to go to the powwow and get culture points— I seriously mean it."

Her mother raised her palms in the air. "For once I have a chance to spend my only sister's birthday with her—"

"Well, what's stopping you?" said Megan. "You guys can go sightseeing. River and I will take the bus back home on Saturday morning. We aren't down for the ferry and the Exploratorium; we want to go to the powwow. We can ride

27

on a bus for a half an hour—come on. We'll get off at the bus stop right in front of Live Oak Park."

Thank you, Megan! River cried out to herself.

"This makes me very cross!" said their mother. "You two agree to weekend plans, then want to change everything—"

"Turn up the sound!" cried their father. "Quick!" The goat was galloping full speed ahead at another, bigger boulder. Megan restored the sound just in time to hear the loud crack of horn against granite. Their father whistled quietly.

"I'm sorry—this I just don't get," Megan announced.

"You don't?" he said. "Billy Whiskers is impressing the gals!"

"By clunking his head on a rock?"

"Yes! The ewes love it! And *that* dude," said their father, "is *one heckuva* heartbreaker. Whoa!" he yelled. Now the goat had rammed a large boulder completely off a cliff. "Did you see that?"

"Honey?" said their mom.

"If *that* can't get the homey a girlfriend," announced their dad, "nothing can!"

River and Megan looked at each other.

The homey? That would immediately be added to the list, along with *dude*.

"Let's get out of here," said Megan. As she and River walked into the kitchen, Megan asked in a low voice, "So. Why do you want to go to the powwow so bad?"

"I love the powwow," said River. "Plus, kids from my class are going. Besides," she added mysteriously, "I have . . . an idea I've been thinking about."

Megan opened the refrigerator and peered up through

28

the clear plastic top shelf. "Anton and I might get matching silver Zuni rings," she whispered. She pulled two bottled lemon ice teas out from behind a carton of milk, a carton of grapefruit juice and a gallon of spring water. "Ha!" she yelled. "We found your hiding place, *Dad*!

"Hang out with me in my room, 'kay?" she asked River.

"I'll be in in a minute," said River. She wandered back and lingered for a moment in the doorway to the living room, casually sipping her iced tea and staring at the tube. The courtship of goats would be out of the question for her Furley report—totally. Now they were scrootching around on their backs in the dust, kicking their hooves in the air. What was the point? "Thanks for the tea, Dad!" River called. Her dad looked over at her and she lifted the bottle in a toast. "Love you!" She scurried away.

Megan was sitting at her desk, digging through a basket of nail polishes. River took a large swallow of tea and looked around. She liked being invited into Megan's room, especially after Megan had just cleaned it up. There were two new posters on the wall: One was of a guy and a girl in swimsuits lying on the beach at the foamy edge of the water, locked in each other's arms. They were both buff— the guy especially. You could see his huge biceps and beautiful shoulders.

River examined him from head to toe. And extremely well-defined calf muscles, she had to admit. She looked back up at his arms, the most scenic part of the poster. Increased muscle development—oh yeah! But something told River biceps like those didn't just automatically come along with Furley's puberty package for boys. "Do you think that guy works out?" River asked.

"E-e-e-e-yeah," said Megan.

The other new poster was a print of a watercolor-and-pen illustration from *Winnie-the-Pooh*. Pooh was watching Christopher Robin tack Eeyore's tail back on with a hammer and nail. Better be careful where you're nailing stuff in *that* vicinity, Christopher!

Under the picture was written: *Friendship is a very comforting sort of thing to have.*

Especially if your friends have good aim! thought River.

Margaret had once given River a card with this very same picture and quote on it, and River had kept it ever since they were in Montessori school together. It was in her box of keepsakes under her bed.

"Guess who has a boyfriend," said River.

"You?" said Megan.

"Nope."

"I don't know but I can tell you this: I wish it would be Aunt Colleen. She better hurry up and hook up with somebody."

"Her ol' biological clock is ticking," said River. "That's what Furball calls it."

"No clock ticking kept Mom from getting pregnant at age forty-something," said Megan. "And she wasn't even trying."

"Right, but at least Mom has a husband."

"Yes, she does," said Megan. "But that's certainly no excuse for completely spacing on birth control—and by the way, what do you think of this *romantic evening* together they're planning at the hotel?"

River stared at her. A romantic evening? With their mom six months pregnant? "What a frightful thought," said River. She decided not to try to picture it.

"So tell me who has a boyfriend," said Megan.

"Margaret," said River.

Megan chuckled. "Margaret," she muttered. "You *must* be kidding."

"She got together with a boy named Noah—at school. In the library."

"No way!"

"She did! By the encyclopedias." River smiled ever so slightly. "They Frenched."

"Now you're lying."

"I know. But they did hold hands under the table in front of the Macs and now they're going out."

"That's cute!"

"I know!"

Megan opened her desk drawer and took out a package of photos in a yellow-and-white envelope. She started looking through them. "I'm getting an eight-by-ten enlargement and a frame for this one," she said, "for Anton for our nine-month anniversary." She handed the photo to River, and River carefully studied it. The picture was of Megan and Anton standing in front of the gazebo in the backyard. Anton's arm was around Megan's waist—and Megan's head was tipped onto his shoulder. Her hand was on Anton's chest, over his heart.

"So you think you and Anton will end up getting married?" asked River.

"*Married?* We're sixteen!" Megan put the photo back in the envelope.

"I didn't mean right away," said River. "I mean—someday."

Megan shrugged.

"I wonder what it would be like to be thirty-something

31

and not be married yet," said River. "I feel sorry for Aunt Colleen. Somebody should hook her up."

"No, somebody should *not*," said Megan sternly. "People should mind their own business. Besides, matchmaking never works out. Couples are meant to find each other or not—nobody can plan destiny, it's impossible!" She reached into a plastic bag of cotton balls. "Somebody's out there for Aunt Colleen right now," she said mysteriously. "They're moving closer and closer together—and they don't even know it." Megan put one foot up on the edge of her chair.

"In the meantime, Aunt Colleen's having a fine time looking all on her own. She probably goes out with cute rich divorced guys who are graying at the temples and wear Armani suits and drive Dodge Vipers. Who buy her roses and forty-dollar bottles of red wine in hopes of scoring."

River's eyes grew rounder. What a shocking thought!

"Only kidding," said Megan. She began sticking cotton between her toes. "But you know what?"

"What?"

"It might help things along if we give Aunt Colleen a makeover for a birthday present," said Megan. "Like they do on *Oprah*. And we'll buy her something sexy from Victoria's Secret. That can't hurt."

"Will you do lipliner and lipstick for me?" said River.

"No. Study your wiener chart."

River wandered into her bedroom. It was neat as a pin; it always was neat as a pin. She flopped onto her bed and looked up at the ceiling. Should she get glow-in-the-dark stars and a moon to stick on up there like Jules had? Or would it just make a mess? Maybe she could line the stars up. Or make a perfect circle of stars, with the moon in the middle.

It was dark outside her window. A big fuzzy moon was rising above the trees. The sky looked a little like the *Starry, Starry Night* painting by Vincent Van Gogh. Would there be any stars to wish on tonight? River hoped so.

She got up to look. A huge, pale moth with feathered antennae began fluttering against the glass. River stared at his plump, furry body. Get away! she scolded him. Nobody sent you signals from here!

Then she quickly closed the blinds in case somebody as nuts as Vincent Van Gogh was peeking in.

River dove back onto her bed. Let's see . . . what should she and Megan pick out for Aunt Colleen's birthday? Maybe they could get her a white Guess? shirt like Kirstin's—or Kirstin's mother's, or whosever it was, or whoever's it was or whomever's—

Learn grammar! River scolded herself. You're practically in the seventh grade!

And get.

Busy.

River fumbled for her pack, dragged it closer to the side of her bed and dug into it with one hand. She pulled out her Human Interaction notebook. She leafed through, stopping at the notes she had made during library time:

JELLYFISH
SEA ANEMONE
WOOD GRUBS
BULBS (?)

Partly because of Georgia O'Keeffe, River loved flowers. Her all-time favorites were the pink naked ladies that bloomed late in summer, on long leafless stems. But the problem with flowers for her report was they reproduced sexually. Bees transported pollen from the sex organs of the male naked ladies to the sex organs of the female naked ladies . . .

Wait a minute! How could there be a male naked lady?

River crossed *BULBS* off her list. Let's see. Maybe sea anemones. They're so prickly! River thought. It's no wonder they don't . . .

She turned to a clean sheet of binder paper and wrote:

River
Mrs. Furley's Class

in the upper right-hand corner. Below it, she added, in perfectly neat script: *The Courtship of Jellyfish.*

No! Too slimy! She erased *Jellyfish* and wrote *the Wood Grub.* There. That was a good enough choice. Her report could be on Bill, the former wood grub she'd had as a pet in Montessori school. She'd liked Bill very much—all the way up until he turned into a dreadful wide-bodied beetle. River slapped the notebook closed.

She dug into her pack and pulled out the envelope containing the guidebook. She located the *Unacceptable Expressions for Adults to Use in the Presence of Preadolescents* paper and added *hoot, the homey, dude, highly irks* and *cross.* Then she fished around through the suggestion papers, to find one DB had written.

Ah.

34

Do not give out extra information was scrawled on a grubby piece of torn paper. *DO NOT ask stuff when friends call.*

The handwriting was unmistakably male. And River had a theory: The tiny hormone messenger guys, the little Captain Testosterones that marched out and told biceps and abs to grow bigger, also blocked the ability of the male's smaller muscles to form proper cursive letters.

She gave DB's suggestion a little teeny-weeny kiss.

Then she opened the rough draft of the guidebook and turned to the list of rules. Because of her mother's behavior this evening, River would need to amend rule number twelve. She chewed on her eraser and wrote: *No unsolicited chats about puberty, male or female.*

Then she slid everything back into the envelope. She put the clasp through the hole and flattened it. If her mother didn't quit committing so many infractions, the little fold-out bendable hasps were going to break right off.

Mothers! What a continuing challenge it was to shape them up and keep them shaped up. It was a thankless, tiresome, never-ending job.

But on the other hand, imagine Margaret—with no mom at all to embarrass her.

Poor Margaret. At age eleven, she needed a stepmom way more than she needed a boyfriend. And Mrs. Furley would be perfect. Perfect!

River felt a twinge of guilt. It seemed that she'd abandoned Margaret lately. She leaned down and slid her treasure box out from underneath her bed. Aha! Right on top, just underneath an oak leaf ironed between two pieces of waxed paper, was the Pooh card Margaret had given her. River opened it up. *DeeR RiVeR*, Margaret had managed to write, with a good deal of erasing—in fact, the paper was almost worn all the way through. *You aR MY FReND. i LoVe You. MaRGaRet R.*

She should show this card to Margaret, for old times' sake. And she should pay more attention to Margaret, and help her snag Furley for a stepmom—if this was possible. Nothing was impossible!

And there was nothing wrong with planning destiny. Megan wasn't a world authority on matchmaking. The courtship of human beings didn't have to depend entirely on nature; it was fine to speed up the process occasionally. Besides, what was so great about courtships in nature? Two smelly goats meet for one romantic encounter; as a result, the female ends up raising a kid while the male goes off to head-butt more rocks. And roll in the dirt. So . . . why not help the natural process along—or even eliminate it altogether?

Margaret's idea of pressuring Furley into calling her dad to discuss the Internet wasn't a bad concept, but people didn't fall for each other on the phone. They had to be lured to the same spot at the same time, to check each other out.

Heh. Heh. River smiled to herself.

River to the rescue! Provided she and Margaret could get out of Saturday's outing with Aunt Colleen . . . River thought through her plan:

On Saturday, at about twelve-thirty or so, she and Megan would take the bus from the city to Live Oak Park and meet Anton at the entrance of the powwow. Of course, Anton and Megan would want to go off by themselves and celebrate their anniversary. Which would be just fine. There would be no need for River to tag along, because

River would have previously arranged to meet Margaret and her dad at the fountain—conveniently located so that River and Margaret could scope out the people as they paid and walked into the entrance of the powwow.

Soon Furley would show up. Margaret and River would wave her over. They'd all chat for a few minutes. Then River and Margaret would accidentally-on-purpose ditch Furley and Margaret's dad. They'd join up with other kids from school—like Noah, Henry, Jules and, most importantly, the Deeb Boy. River put her hand over her heart and lightly patted it. Down, girl. Focus on the plan, she told herself.

Meanwhile, back at the ranch, Gladys Furley and Margaret's dad would be together at the powwow—separated from the main group. They'd do the smart thing: stay in one place. The two of them would sit on the lawn, share a piece of fry bread sprinkled with confectioner's sugar or have an Indian taco, if it didn't make too much of a mess.

Were plastic forks and knives available at the Indian taco stand?

They'd better be.

Hopefully Mrs. Furley would look really good—wearing something springish, but not sleeveless. Maybe she'd have her nails done—a French manicure . . . A breeze would stir in her hair and rustle in her blouse and flash glimpses of her cleavage . . .

What a great scenario River was concocting! It made her happy just to dream it up. She found a pen and wrote *River River River River River* diagonally across the front of her Human Interaction notebook. What a distinguished signature she had—perfect for an artist, and almost impossible to forge. She signed *River River River River River* below the other *River*s. Then she drew a heart and wrote a very teensy *River + DB* inside.

Get busy! she told herself. She circled the heart and made it the center of a daisy and drew petals around it, a stem and two leaves. Nobody would know who lived inside that flower but her. Homework! I mean it!

River heaved a tremendous sigh. Obviously, to help Margaret, she'd have to stick out Sex Ed. She didn't really want to apply to work in the office anyway, since Stella was one of Mrs. Bagley's office assistants. There was no one River less wanted to deal with than Stella—except, of course, Kirstin.

So River would continue to study how humans interact along with the rest of her classmates—except that River's study would now include the fieldwork necessary to encourage interaction between Jim Rothrock and Gladys Furley at the powwow in the park.

River stood up and reached into her wastebasket. She found and unrumpled the cross-section, side-view diagram of the male getup. She stared at it for a long moment. Then she closed her eyes and shook her head.

Gosh.

What an impractical design.

Four

OH! MYGOSH.

River stared at Mrs. Furley's hands, folded prettily in her lap, as she sat on Mr. Elmo's desktop. What was the woman—psychic? She'd gotten a French manicure! This was *definitely* a sign. River should get down to business and help Margaret with the powwow hookup plan. Pronto.

"As girls are prowling through lingerie departments," began Mrs. Furley slowly, "contemplating bras that clip in the front, bras that clasp in the back, clipless, claspless bras that you pull over your head, bras with underwires, sports bras, sports bras with underwires *et cetera!*" Mrs. Furley pretended to have completely run out of breath. She inhaled deeply before she continued. "What personal item might a *boy* be shopping for?"

The class was quiet.

"If this boy were planning to participate in sports?"

Mrs. Furley looked around at the faces of the students. "Hel-lo out there!" she said after a while. "Anybody home?"

Nobody spoke.

"Any ideas on what boys would be shopping for?"

"Cleats," said DB.

"And what else?" said Mrs. Furley. "That might go along with cleats?"

"Socks," said Noah.

"Boys? Oi yoi yoi. Come on now!" She slapped her forehead. "What might you need along with cleats and socks to protect yourselves while playing ball?"

Mrs. Furley looked from student to student. "You don't remember our discussion? Didn't everyone get one of these last Friday?" She held up a cross-section, side-view labeled diagram titled REVIEW: THE MALE REPRODUCTIVE SYSTEM.

"Unfortunately, yes," mumbled Jules. And she and River exchanged pained expressions.

Mrs. Furley went into her lecture mode: "Well, *as* you all know, males, *like* females, have internal and external sex organs." She stopped. "Anybody want to name them, without looking at your diagrams?"

Now *this* was an offer anybody could refuse.

Mrs. Furley looked hopefully around the room. "Internal and external—somebody give it a go.

"Nobody?"

Nope.

Nobody was interested in naming the male reproductive organs without using a diagram—and nobody was interested in naming them using a diagram either. Nobody was interested in naming even one of the male reproductive organs.

"How 'bout just the external ones, then?"

No! Was she kidding? Those were the worst!

At least girls kept their sex organs pretty much up inside their bodies, where they belonged.

"Okay," said Mrs. Furley. "But remember: You *will* be responsible for knowing those labels. As I warned you on Friday, I could give a pop quiz on that particular diagram at any time. So study up."

Oooohyeah. We'll all just be studyin' up a storm, thought River.

Mrs. Furley eased off the desktop, straightened her suit jacket and strolled past the blackboard, gathering her thoughts. She looked stylish today, except that the gold buttons on her jacket made her look like a bellboy in a fancy hotel.

River quietly sighed. That's where *she* would be on Friday—in a fancy hotel, instead of at All-Stars practice with just about every other sixth-grader in the district. She glanced at DB. She hoped no other sixth-grade girls would be scoping *him* out.

Her heart skipped a beat. Would Kirstin be going?

"Now. Here's what I'm getting at," said Mrs. Furley. "A comparison. We've been through breast buds and bras, periods and pads, and the question *is*," she said, drawing out the *is,* "What comparison can we make between what happens to *a boy* as *he* approaches puberty—and what happens to a girl?"

Why was *this* the question? River didn't recall anyone

asking this annoying question, unless Margaret had put it in the question box.

"What kinds of things does *he* have to deal with?" asked Mrs. Furley.

Sex Ed classes, thought River.

"What are some of *his* concerns?" said Mrs. Furley. "Let's compare. A boy's reproductive system, just like a girl's, begins to mature according to his own unique and special timetable. So the onset of puberty varies from male to male. In most cases, it begins at about age—what? Anybody remember?" The class was quiet. "We've been over this before. Nobody?"

Mrs. Furley gazed around the room.

"At about age *twelve*," she said, with just a slight hint of irritation. "And *as* with a girl, changes begin to occur that are both emotional and physical." Mrs. Furley paused. "Let's chat for a moment about the physical changes," she chirped, as if this were just the best, most fabulous idea in the world.

Let's not, thought River.

"Like girls'," continued Mrs. Furley, "boys' systems are regulated by *hormones,* which act as? River?"

Yikes!

"Messengers," said River quickly.

"Right you are!" said Mrs. Furley. "Hormones act as messengers to signal changes within the body. Changes like hairs sprouting under the armpits—" Mrs. Furley lifted her left arm as though she were doing a pirouette and pointed to her armpit, Vanna White style.

River closed her eyes. Don't look at any boy, she told herself sternly. But she had an irresistible urge just to steal one tiny peek at the Deeb, and she did. He was slumped in his chair, with his elbow on his desktop and his fist in his cheek—staring at the clock.

"—and the beginning of underarm perspiration, and growing thicker leg hairs—" said Mrs. Furley.

"Mrs. Furley?" interrupted Margaret. "Wait. Is each individual hair thicker?"

"God in heaven!" cried Kirstin. "I can't take this anymore." She buried her head in her arms, which were extended across the top of her desk with her fingers dangling over the edge. She peered over her elbow at Stella.

Where did Kirstin get such a great color of nail polish? River wondered. She must have swiped it from her mom.

"Kirstin?" said Mrs. Furley. "Can it."

Can it. Now this River hadn't heard in years. Add it to the list, she told herself. Along with *oi yoi yoi* and *give it a go.*

"Thicker hair shafts," said Mrs. Furley in a puzzled way. "Good question, Margles, but I don't know the answer. I only know that at the onset of puberty boys begin to get, well, woolier! Then there's the lowering of the voice, the increased muscle development and the growth of the exterior reproductive organs—"

River flinched. Now she really *really* was not going to look at any boy, not one. She stared at her desktop.

"—that are also in the package."

"They're in a *package*?" said Margaret.

"I mean—that are in this whole puberty pack I'm describing—for boys."

"Oh," said Margaret.

"But I guess we *could* say that two of the exterior reproductive organs actually *are* in a package, of sorts," Mrs.

43

Furley said in a cheery voice. "In a sac, called the . . . ?" Not one person in the class even looked in her direction. "Scrotum," said Mrs. Furley, to answer her own question.

Help! Here she goes again!

"But we've already talked enough about scrotums," said Mrs. Furley.

I'll say, thought River. We'd talked enough about scrotums before we'd even talked about scrotums once!

"Which brings us back around to my original query: What do boys wear to protect themselves? Come *on* now. What should a boy wear when playing sports? To protect a most extremely critical area of the anatomy? That should never be allowed to suffer an impact? Noah?"

"A batting helmet," said Noah.

"Right," said Mrs. Furley. "But I'm talking about the southerly regions of the body, Noah—things below the belt." She looked around the room. "Anybody want to help him out here?"

The class was so quiet that River could plainly hear the faint sound of some primary students playing their plastic recorders all the way from the multipurpose room.

"Who would you like to help you, Noah?" asked Mrs. Furley gently.

Noah looked at Henry, who ducked behind his desktop. Noah pointed at DB.

Mrs. Furley smiled. "Tell us, Deeb. You play baseball, don't you? Aren't you catcher?"

"Uh—yeah," said DB.

"Then tell us."

"Well," began DB. "In order to protect things in . . . the southerly region, as you call it . . ."

Uh-oh. River's heart raced. Would he really say it?

44

"A guy needs to wear . . ."

River held her breath.

"Shin guards," said DB.

Mrs. Furley nodded. "Right. And how's about an *athletic supporter,* boys? And a *cup* to slip into it?"

River thought a minute. A jockstrap with a cup inside? Now, this was a new one. What *kind* of a cup? It couldn't be like a teacup or a mug. She tried to picture the setup. It must have sort of an underwearish look about it—like a thong with a Slurpee lid tucked into the front.

Would it have a clasp in the front? Or the back? Did the boy step into it? Or did he just pull it down over his head?

River glanced at Jules, who was looking at Henry, who was sitting with his hand shielding his eyes from everyone.

Could it be? Henry, *embarrassed*? He was faking it!

"I know you're staring at me," said Henry without looking up. "The girls are staring at us!" he told Mrs. Furley.

"Oh, they are not. And the girls had to put up with all kinds of nonsense and silliness from you when we were studying girl stuff."

"No, they didn't."

"Yes, they did. Last class, I heard you whispering about bird breasts. What goes around comes around, my friend," said Mrs. Furley cheerily. She looked at the clock. "And that about winds it up for today. Mr. Elmo will be returning any minute. Any questions? Did everybody write down the Brain Tickler? Extra credit, remember."

River looked up at the Brain Tickler Mrs. Furley had written on the board. Oh.

My.

Gosh.

This one took the cake. It had been bad enough having to fill out worksheets and diagrams. But really.

River threw her pencil into her desk.

What a question.

Five

MRS. FURLEY PACKED UP her things and waved to Mr. Elmo as he wandered back into the room. He pointed to the powwow flyer. "Yes, I noticed," said Mrs. Furley. "Are you and Mrs. Elmo going?"

"E-e-e-eyou betcha."

You betcha. List it! River told herself.

But see? Mrs. Furley was being drawn to the powwow without any outside influence. Hmmmm. Maybe River should let nature take its course.

"See you soon," Mrs. Furley told the class. She paused for a minute in the doorway and did an extended prom-queen wave in slow motion.

Ridiculous!

"Remember," she sang out, "courtship behaviors in the animal kingdom! It's not just moths who use their legs

47

to attract mates!" She lifted her pants leg above her ankle and pointed her toe. Then she vamped out of the room.

What a psycho! But a lovable, funny one. Sort of.

River watched Mr. Elmo rearrange a few things on his desktop. Good Old Elmo Boy! Straightening up after Mrs. Messmaker. She probably wrinkled his blotter with her ample derriere.

"I almost forgot again!" said Noah suddenly. "Mr. Elmo? I have input—for the limos. I thought of this last night . . . I'm afraid I'll forget it again."

"We couldn't get that lucky," mumbled Stella.

"Okay," began Noah. "Everyone in the limo group is getting a disposable camera, right?"

Kirstin forced a huge yawn, and patted it.

"Instead, why doesn't Stella's mom just buy one keepable camera for Stella?" said Noah. "And then buy film and have everybody take turns?"

Kirstin closed her eyes, tipped her head forward and pretended to snore.

"All that plastic and cardboard," continued Noah, "all that packaging just being thrown out. And for what purpose? When it's over, nobody even owns a camera."

"Hmmmmm," said Mr. Elmo. "Not a bad idea."

"Take a cue," whispered Kirstin. "Nobody's interested in your little environmentally conscious PC suggestions."

"Go play tonsil hockey with Margaret," whispered Stella.

"Maybe the limo group will want to consider it after lunch," said Mr. Elmo. "At guidebook time."

"I *don't* think so," whispered Kirstin.

"Mr. Elmo?" said Jules. "We need guidebook time extended again."

Mr. Elmo lowered his chin and looked at Jules over the top of his glasses. *"You do?"*

Jules nodded. "Mrs. Furley dumped another huge last-minute assignment on us. About how certain living things . . ." Jules paused, searching for the right words.

"Why not negotiate this later?" said Mr. Elmo, glancing at the clock. "Hot lunchers?" he barked. "Line up. On the double! But Jules? Come on up here for a minute, would you?"

Here we go again, thought River.

DB walked over to River's desk. "You going to the pow-wow?" he asked. River's heart did a little flip.

"I'm trying to work it out with my mom and dad. I might have to visit with my aunt instead. Are you going?"

DB nodded. "With Henry. He *has* to. He's got a D in social studies."

"That's no good," said River.

"Is Jules going?" said DB. He lowered his voice. "Henry wants to know."

"He asked you to ask me?" whispered River.

Kirstin had paused nearby and was leaning down to tie her shoe. What a horrid spy! She stood up and tugged on the front of her blouse to straighten it. River simply did *not* understand how Kirstin suddenly had such sizable hooters—or honkers, or whatever Henry called them. Suddenly she was built like a Barbie doll!

"Deeb!" called Kirstin, and DB looked over at her. Kirstin carefully pinched a very small piece of lint off her shirt pocket.

What a weasel! She probably put it there, thought River.

"What?" asked DB.

Kirstin glanced over her shoulder at Mr. Elmo and then lowered her voice. "Can you and Henry score some ticket stubs for me and my limo buds?"

DB shrugged. "How am I supposed to do that?"

"Duh! Snag 'em from people once they're in!" whispered Kirstin. Her eyes twinkled.

River couldn't believe Kirstin's mother let her wear eye shadow, eyeliner and mascara to school in the sixth grade!

"Why can't you guys get 'em yourself?" DB asked.

Kirstin moved one fist up on her hip. "Somehow, Deeb, I just can't see me and my limo buds chillin' at a powwow."

"I'll see what I can do," said DB. He turned his back on Kirstin and spoke quietly to River. "So ask Jules if she's coming, okay?"

"I'll talk to her about it," said River.

"Thanks," said DB. He headed out of the classroom and River watched him go. What a sweetie . . .

Kirstin brushed up against him accidentally-on-purpose as they walked together through the doorway. Then she stopped suddenly so DB would bump into her. What a dreadful rat!

River looked over to see if Jules had taken any of this in.

Jules hadn't. She was looking at the ceiling as Mr. Elmo lectured her. "You ask for more time, yet you conveniently never have time for me to take a good look at your group's notes," Mr. Elmo was telling her. "It's tough to be a parent! That should be acknowledged. Don't you think?"

"Not really," said Jules.

"Well, I'll tell you one thing: I think this idea for a

citation booklet to go along with each guidebook is going a bit too far."

"Actually, we credit you with that concept," said Jules. "We hadn't even thought of it until the other afternoon when you said our guidebook made us seem more like cops than kids."

"I regret that statement deeply," said Mr. Elmo. "But regardless, I'd like to look over your materials again. Who's in possession of the notes at the moment?"

River hurried out of the room and lingered against the breezeway wall, out of sight of Mr. Elmo.

"Deeb said Henry wants you to come to the powwow," River told Jules as soon as she walked out the classroom door.

Jules brought her hand to her mouth. Her eyes widened. "He *did*?"

"Don't touch your face!" River told her. "You're breaking *YM*'s Number One Clean Skin Rule!"

River pulled Jules along by her sweatshirt sleeve.

Kirstin, Stella and their limo-party groupies had already nabbed the only shaded picnic table. Kirstin, wearing shorts, had knotted her shirt above her belly button and was displaying more than the maximum amount of skin allowable at school. She was sitting on the tabletop, leaning back with her arms extended, her hands folded under one knee and her toe pointed, Marilyn Monroe style.

How long had she practiced *this* pose?

River sat with Jules under an old shade tree whose leaves were newly hatched. A breeze lifted the branches. Yikes! She hoped nothing to do with tree sex would flutter or plop down on top of her or get on her lunch. She sat up straight and cautiously opened her bag and peered in.

"Thanks to Mrs. Furball, boysenberries will never again be anything but little fat purple sex organs that hang off a bush. Henry!" she called. She reached into the bag and held up her yogurt. "Want this?"

River glanced at Jules. "This is for your benefit," she whispered.

Henry wandered over. "Here," said River.

The girls watched as he ripped off the foil lid, tipped back his head and tapped the bottom of the container, dumping the yogurt into his mouth. He wiped off his mouth, chin and nose with his sleeve.

"Catch!" said Jules. She tossed him an apricot and he split it open, picked out the pit and stuffed both halves of the apricot into his mouth.

"You just ate a tree organ," River told him. "But never mind. Tell DB that Jules *is* going to the powwow on Saturday."

"I am?" said Jules. She casually looked in another direction.

"Yes, she is," River told Henry.

Henry booted the tree trunk a couple of times. Then he jammed his hands deep into his pockets and walked away, kicking the apricot pit ahead of him as he went.

The kids were noisy as they came in from lunch, and Mr. Elmo erased two points from the blackboard. Now they were two points further away from an outing at the Community Center. Would they get there before June?

Henry grabbed DB's cap and tossed it in the direction of the wastebasket.

Not at this rate.

Mr. Elmo capped the marker. "So. ___
he announced. "Everybody ready? Wiggle
bunny noses if you're ready." He twitched h___

The kids groaned and Mr. Elmo chuckle___
"Before we begin," he began, "let me remind y___
time: Do your best. Make each and every one of u___ ___of
our class effort. How does the saying go?" Nobody answered. "About doing our best? Deeb? We reviewed this
recently. 'Good, better, best. Never let it rest. Until the
good is better. And the better—'? Say it," said Mr. Elmo.

"You say it!" said DB. "I forget."

"No, you don't!"

"Yes, I do."

"Best," said Kirstin. She inspected her nail polish.

"Good girl. Some of these old sayings are pretty pro-
found, and there's no harm in learning a few. Want to
know one I memorized when I was your age?"

Kirstin stared at her nails and mouthed the words:
"Not *r-r-really.*"

"My sixth-grade teacher taught it to us. What was her
name? Anyway: 'Love many, trust few. Always paddle your
own canoe.' "

"That's not very community oriented," said Margaret.

"Well, it may not be, but I consider it darn good advice," said Mr. Elmo. He scratched the top of his head.
"What was that teacher's name?"

"Well, whatever it was, it's actually kind of a paranoid
approach to life when you think about it," said Noah.

"No, it isn't. Miss Hirl!" cried Mr. Elmo. "Her name
was Miss Wanda Hirl—I'll never forget that woman."

Henry looked up with a frightened expression. "The
woman's name was Wanda Hirl?"

_s."

"It *was?*"

Henry looked sideways at DB. "Say 'Wanda Hirl' five times fast," he whispered. DB and several other students around him began repeating it quietly to themselves.

River heard two little snorts come out of somebody.

"DB?" said Mr. Elmo. "Get out from behind that desk lid. I know you're laughing. Jules? Knock it off! Jeepers creepers!"

River wrote *knock it off* and *jeepers creepers* on her desktop in pencil.

"Sorry, Mr. Elmo," said DB. "But you do have to admit—your teacher *did* have kind of an unusual name."

"All of you get to work," said Mr. Elmo.

Kids got up and quietly began arranging themselves in clusters. Margaret, Noah, Henry, Jules and DB gathered in the back of the room.

Henry found it convenient to stand close to Jules and look over her shoulder as she pretended to be interested in the terrarium.

River busily transferred the unacceptable expressions from her desktop onto the list in the guidebook folder. Then she licked her finger and rubbed away the evidence. She glanced up at Mr. Elmo. He was looking in the direction of her group with a sour expression.

She tossed her hair over her shoulder and walked to the back of the room.

"I have something to add to the rules," called Henry.
"What is it?"

"Last night," said Henry, "my mom started breakdancing in the mall and—"

Jules made a little gasping sound. "I'd just lay down

54

and die," she whispered with her hand on her throat, "if my mom did that."

"*Lie* down and die," said a voice behind them.

Margaret whipped her head around and glared at Mr. Elmo. "You said you wouldn't interfere!" she scolded. "Can you please stop being Mr. Grammar Cop for just a few minutes? We're brainstorming here!"

"Still *brainstorming*? These books are a week short of going to press! What's with this group, pray tell?"

"*Pray tell,*" muttered River. She carefully wrote this onto the bottom of the unacceptable list while Mr. Elmo watched.

"Can we have a little privacy?" said Noah. "Seriously."

Mr. Elmo walked away, muttering. "I just think it's an obnoxious approach to a darn good assignment. Kids these days—handing out citations to their hardworking parents. It wouldn't have happened in my day, I can tell ya that!"

"Okay," said River. "No breakdancing—but wouldn't rule two already cover it?"

"What's rule two?" said Henry.

Jules sighed very, *very* deeply. "You *wrote* rule two."

"I *did*?"

Jules gently elbowed him and he stumbled backward into a chair and fell down on purpose with a great clatter.

"That guidebook darn well better be good and it darn well better be ready by the deadline!" called Mr. Elmo. "It's fifty percent of your final grade in language arts, don't forget."

Jules went into administrative mode. "Get up," she told Henry. "You jerk. And let's review all the rules. Margaret? Read." She took the folder from River and handed it to Margaret, who opened it and began to read:

"Number one: No parent shall wear a cowboy hat with the exception of a parent who actually is in a rodeo."

Margaret stopped. "But cowboy *boots* are okay, aren't they?"

Nobody answered.

"Boots are fine," lied River.

"Read!" Jules told Margaret.

"Parent shall get prior approval for any clothing featuring palm trees and sunsets. No bowling shirts. No neon accessories. No pulling up cuffs of sweats and hiking up socks and then forgetting to put pants legs down again. Also, see additional rule number four.

"Number two. No parent shall dance, either separately or together, to any music at any time, including when alone at home. This means you! *No parent shall sing, hum or whistle along with any sound system, including sound systems not yet invented. Parent should not bob head, tap furniture or make any other rhythmic movements that could be construed as dance-related.* Especially no neck and shoulder involvement. No beat boxing!!!

"Number three. No parent shall tell a joke to any friend or acquaintance of kid. Tip: A joke, once told, does not grow funnier with more telling. Give it a rest!

"Number four. Parents shall not hold up clothing and say: 'How's about this?' in any clothing store. No fidgeting with kid's clothes—no flatten-

ing collars, etc. Hands off! No parent shall yell to kid in mall. No parent shall run in the mall.

"*Run only on the track, or in the neighborhood, and only if properly dressed for running. Which means Nikes, Adidas, or other presently acceptable running shoes,* matching *white socks, sweats (preferred colors: gray, black, navy). No hiking waistband up or allowing sweats to become off-center.*

"*Number five. No parent shall attempt to hold hands with kid at the mall. Parent shall not attempt to kiss kid within one thousand feet of any mall, school, movie theater, theme park or home of other kid. No parent shall honk and wave goodbye to kid. Tip: After dropping kid off, leave the area quickly and quietly. No parent shall appear in public behind the wheel of a convertible more than ten years old, unless the car is more than thirty years old and restored to showroom standards. Hydraulics okay.*

"*Number six. No parent shall yell encouragement during any sporting event at which kid is participating or is present as spectator. No parent shall cry during singing of patriotic songs; no parent shall display emotion during kid's choral or instrumental performances.*

"*Number seven. When kid's friends are over, no parent shall converse unnecessarily with any friend of their kid. No saying hello to kid's friend(s) unless kid is present. All conversations shall be kept to an absolute minimum. Tip: Be courteous, but minimally.* No questions! *No parent shall carry on phone conversation with any friend of kid. Tip:*

Keep it brief. Give information—don't get information.

"Number eight. Absent an emergency situation, or unless delivering a snack, a parent shall not enter a kid's room. Stand in doorway to speak; if door is closed or partially closed, move close to door and speak or speak through crack. Tip: Leave clean laundry in basket outside door. Fold laundry. No parent shall deviate from explicit instructions about snack orders. Tip: If you're not going to prepare food as per instructions, then don't offer snacks at all. If a kid's friend is over, no parent shall fry, bake, boil, broil, steam or sauté eggplant, mushrooms, cauliflower, squash, clams, oysters, squid or organ meats in home of kid without the explicit approval of kid. No parent shall offer cheese that stinks to a kid's friend(s). No loud chewing.*

"Number nine. No parent shall squeeze the cheese and say oops. No dad shall say, 'Pull on my finger!'*

"Number ten. No rubbernecking. If someone or something is pointed out by kid to parent, be cool.*

"Number eleven. If a kid asks if there is any toilet paper on back of pants, shorts, skirt or shoes, just drop back and look while kid proceeds casually to walk ahead. Tip: Just say yes or no.* This is not joke time. *Answer the question. Do not repeat the question.*

"Number twelve. No parent shall ask any questions about Human Interaction class. Nor shall any parent spontaneously volunteer information*

*about any aspect of the human reproductive process
or of any mammal, bird or insect or fish, amphibian
or arachnid. No unsolicited chats about puberty,
male or female.*

*"Number thirteen. No attempts to talk teen
talk. Never use expressions outside of your own
generational group, and use your own such expressions sparingly. Example: Limit use of the word
groovy. Don't say 'Far out.' Never, ever say 'I
hafta take a whiz.' "*

"Then we add the rest of the list," said River. "Under
the separate heading of . . ." She displayed the Unacceptable Expressions paper. "Anyone have anything else
to add?"

The kids studied it for a moment.

"No saying 'What up,' " said DB.

River wrote it down.

"No saying ' 'sup,' either."

River added it.

"Anything else?"

The group studied the list for several minutes.

"Are you *sure* it's okay to wear cowboy boots?" said
Margaret.

Nobody answered.

"I guess we're done then," said River.

"You do the final *final* editing," Jules told River. "Just
keep it out of Mr. Elmo's hands and get it to me by the
powwow, at the very latest. I have to have it Saturday, to
type it into my dad's computer when I go there on Sunday."

"I might not be able to go to the powwow!" cried River.

"Yes, you will," said DB. "Tell your mom and dad you *have to*." He turned to Jules. "River will be there."

Henry lifted up Jules's ponytail and looked underneath.

Jules slugged him.

"And she'll also design the cover," said DB. "Won't ya, Riv." He leaned his elbow on River's shoulder and turned his head to look at her.

Yikes! thought River.

DB's face was six inches away from her earlobe! Why hadn't she remembered to polish her earrings with the little flannel silver-polishing rag?

Six

THROUGHOUT THE REST of the school day, River replayed this moment in her head. The Deeb's face—so close to her cheek. And ear!

She *wished* she'd polished her earrings, and she *wished* she'd used Megan's apricot sea kelp facial cleanser—or better yet, a Perfect Pore cleansing strip.

Your pores are perfectly fine! she told herself as she boarded the school bus for the long ride home. She walked down the aisle and chose an empty seat about halfway back.

"Do I smell good?" River asked Margaret as soon as Margaret sat down beside her.

"Yup."

"What do I smell like?"

Margaret tipped closer. She took a deep, slow breath. "I think mint."

"Good."

Margaret took another whiff. "But it's kind of subtle. Why?"

"Just wondering," said River.

She would have preferred Margaret to smell a spring bouquet, but mint at least was better than the musty natural aroma that might have wafted out from under River's armpits if she hadn't been policing them.

The bus rumbled out of the parking lot onto Adobe Road.

"Do you think I'm being too obvious?" said Margaret.

River stared at the back of the bus seat. "Too obvious about what?"

Margaret chuckled softly to herself. "Good," she said. "If you didn't notice, I'm sure nobody else picked up on it." She put her hand on the crystal that hung on a gold chain around her neck and closed her eyes. A smile crept across her face.

"Something about Noah?" said River.

Margaret shook her head.

River stared at Margaret's profile—at her rosebud mouth and perfect nose, a nose as perfect as the picture of the girl in the "Draw Me" contest in the back of *Reader's Digest* magazine.

"Oh, you mean Furley and your dad," said River. "No, I don't think you're being too obvious. In fact, I've been cooking up a plan to help you."

Margaret slowly raised her hand in the air to indicate "stop." Then she said, "I'm not ready to hear it yet. Today I've been visualizing Mrs. Furley and my dad as a couple. First, I meditate." She gently gripped her necklace again.

"I am a hollow reed . . . I am a hollow reed . . . I am a hollow reed," she whispered.

"You'll be asleep in five minutes," River told her. "And you won't hear my seriously good plan. It involves—"

Margaret put her finger to her lips.

River looked at her watch. "You'll be out like a rock in five minutes; I'm timing you." It was three-ten.

River turned her head and looked out the window.

Margaret Rothrock, the Crystal Wacko Visualizer. What good could meditating and visualizing do to put two people together?

What a hippie Margaret was!

A few minutes later, River quietly turned and peered at Margaret. She studied Margaret's eyelids; they were still. Air was softly moving between Margaret's lips. Her hand had relaxed. The crystal was catching the sunlight; it made a rainbow pattern on Margaret's fingers.

River's thoughts strayed to the weekend.

Would Kirstin and Stella be going to watch the All-Stars players practice on Friday after school or not? Of course they would! And on Saturday, they would show up at the powwow in miniskirts and seduce DB into passing them ticket stubs through the fence. For the whole limo group!

To make matters worse, DB and Kirstin were neighbors. Sometimes their moms carpooled! River sat there imagining Kirstin and DB sitting in the backseat of Kirstin's mom's new Lexus. By the time the bus driver pulled over to her stop, River was fuming.

Under other circumstances, she would have been happy that her dad was home early and waiting for her on the corner. "Hi, sweetie!" he called as she stepped onto the sidewalk. "How's my girl?"

"Where's Mom?" snapped River.

"Having a snack. Why?"

"I need to talk to her about Saturday."

They walked toward home. "Well, you know," said her father gently, "she's pretty disappointed that you girls want to bail out of our Saturday plans with Aunt Colleen."

"Is Megan home?" said River.

"No."

"Great," said River sarcastically.

She walked ahead of her father. "What's the rush?" he called.

"Who's rushing?" cried River. She rushed up the path and took the steps up onto the porch two at a time. "Mom?" she shouted through the screen. "I absolutely, positively can*not* stay in the city all day Saturday with you and Dad and Aunt Colleen. I can't!"

"What?" called her mother.

River stormed into the house. She flung her backpack in the corner of the hallway, near the hat rack by the door. She stormed into the kitchen. "I—can—not—go—to—the—Ex—plor—a—tor—i—um!" she said in a clipped voice, as if her mother were unable to understand English.

"Calm down," said her mother. "What's wrong with you?"

"What's wrong with *me*?" said River. She stared at her mother. "I'm not the one eating a banana and peanut butter sandwich with honey in it."

"These were very popular in the sixties," said River's mom. "Want a bite?"

"No!"

River's mom sank her teeth into the sandwich. "Are you sure?" she said with her mouth full. She closed her eyes. "Mmmmmm—mmmmm!"

River stalked over to the counter and yanked a paper towel off the roll. "Here! There's honey all over your chin."

"Sit down and calm down," said her mother. She took a large swallow of milk and dabbed at her chin. "And tell me what's going on."

"What's going on is that I need to go to the powwow in the park on Saturday and I need to be there before one o'clock."

"Why?"

"To meet with my guidebook group! We have a guidebook to finish—in case you didn't know."

"At a powwow? I thought your guidebook was a rulebook for parents."

"It is!" cried River. "Don't you think there are rules for parents at public events? Like powwows?"

Her mother shrugged.

"There are more rules for parents at public events than there are for parents anyplace else in the world!" said River. "And anyway, I *have* to deliver my *fully edited* notes to the group leader at the powwow."

"Who's the group leader?"

"Jules! There's a piece of napkin paper stuck to your chin!"

"Heaven forbid," said River's mother. She rolled it onto her fingers and dropped it onto her plate. River stared at it with a disgusted expression.

"Tell me," said River's mother slyly. "Who's in your group?" She moved her tongue to the corner of her mouth to hide a smile. "Besides Jules?"

"Look!" said River. "Can Megan and I take the bus to Live Oak Park on Saturday morning or not? Just tell me now. I want to know if I'm going to flunk social studies because of not getting culture points."

River's mom ran her finger around the edge of her sandwich, scooping up a blob of honey. "Flunk social studies," she whispered. She stuck her finger into her mouth. "My straight-A student?"

River said nothing.

"Any of these kids you *have* to meet—boys?" asked her mother.

"No!" said River. She marched out of the kitchen and into her room, slamming the door behind her. This was a trick of Megan's, and River hoped it would work.

She sat on the edge of her bed. She heard her mother get up and go out the front door. She tiptoed to the window and spied on her parents, who were talking quietly on the lawn. Both parents stood for a moment, shaking their heads. She saw her mother fling her arms into the air.

"Okay, okay," River's mom called to her through the bedroom door a moment later. "You two win. We lose. You can come out now."

River walked quietly into the hall. Don't smile, she told herself.

Her parents were looking at her with serious expressions. "But there will be rules," said her dad. "One of us, or Colleen, will walk you and Megan to the Golden Gate Transit station. It's near the hotel, just across Market, so we'll see that you get on the right bus."

"You and Megan will sit in the front, close to the driver," said River's mother. "The bus station is where the route originates, so you'll be the first ones on, and you'll have a good choice of seats."

River took a very, very long, deep breath and exhaled noisily through her mouth.

"You two ride for thirty minutes, without talking to anybody else except the driver," continued her mother. "We'll tell the driver what stop you get off, when you board."

What? thought River. Now a sixteen-year-old and a twelve-year-old are incapable of getting off a bus?

Say nothing, she instructed herself. Look deeply into her eyes as if you are listening very carefully and taking all of this in . . .

"You'll get off at Live Oak Park, right there by the entrance."

"Okay," said River in a respectful way.

"It's broad daylight, and the powwow will be in full swing," said River's dad. "I'm sure you'll manage to arrive just fine."

"Thanks, Dad," said River.

"I'll miss you," he said stoically. "And I'll miss the powwow.

"Fisherman's Wharf on a Saturday," he mumbled as he walked away, "with two crackpot sisters, one six months pregnant. God help me!"

River's mother waved her into the kitchen. She held up the sandwich. River hesitated, then leaned forward and took a small bite.

"I was once in the sixth grade too," her mother said quietly.

What was that supposed to mean?

"And we also had a group project to complete. Naturally, the girls arranged it so that a few cute boys would work with us. We chose to do a statistics problem. Something to do with how many bowling pins got knocked down in a certain number of games." She chuckled to herself. "So of course we had to have meetings at the local bowling alley."

River took another small bite.

"I liked a boy named Dicky Dingman."

"Great, Mom," said River. "Could you make me one of those sandwiches, with less peanut butter and more honey?"

"You don't want to hear about Dicky Dingman and me?"

"And a glass of milk," said River. "You can just set it on the table by my bed. I've got homework. I have to memorize a very complex diagram."

"And how we shared one strawberry milk shake?"

"No!" cried River.

What was the matter with the woman?

What a disgusting image: her mother exchanging strawberries, milk, vanilla ice cream and spit with a boy named Dicky Dingman.

Seven

"I'M NOT SAYING any girl or woman should *want* one," whispered Margaret. "I am only saying that many points could be brought up. On both sides."

"Please leave me alone, Margaret," said River. "I mean it." She looked out the bus window. They were still miles from school and Margaret was making the rumbling, rambling, rotten trip even longer.

"I realize the survey is a little avant-garde," said Margaret, "but—"

"Margaret?" said River quietly. "Like I told you: I wouldn't want one for any reason. Okay? So drop it."

"Okay," said Margaret. "But did you figure out Mrs. Furley's Brain Tickler yet?"

"No. And I don't want any extra credit."

"Well, I'll tell you the reason why one of the deeley boppers is lower than the other one—"

"This I don't need to know," said River.

"It's so they don't crash into each other when the man is running."

Crash? thought River. "Oh," she said.

"If they were side by side," continued Margaret, "they'd crush each other."

Ouch, thought River. Even a girl could relate to that!

"And get smooshed!" said Margaret.

"Okay!" said River. "I get it!"

"My cousin Helen helped me figure it out. But Riv? If you haven't settled on a topic yet, I'd like to invite you to coauthor my survey. We could be a research team. Collaboration!"

River closed her eyes. "*No* thank you," she said. She opened her eyes and looked sideways at Margaret. "I'm going to go with the ol' wood grub."

"Wood grub? *Why?*"

"Well, one reason is because of Bill."

"Bill!" cried Margaret. "I remember that guy from Montessori school!"

"And the other, more important reason is, wood grubs don't . . ." She moved closer to Margaret. ". . . have sex," she whispered into Margaret's ear.

"They don't?" said Margaret quietly.

River shook her head.

"I don't blame them," said Margaret. She looked down at the notebook on her lap. She had divided the page with a vertical line. On one side of the line was written *Pros*, on the other, *Cons*. "Are you *sure* you don't want to take just a moment or two of your time and fill this out?"

"I'm positive," said River.

"For example, it *might* be a handy thing to have on a picnic," said Margaret.

"No, it wouldn't," said River.

"Or to take along on a hike," said Margaret.

River ignored her.

"Well, then I'll just interview myself."

"Go for it," said River.

Margaret carefully wrote *Convenient for outdoor excursions* under the *Pros* category. Then she drummed her fingers on her knee. "What else?" she whispered to herself.

"Nothing else!" said River.

"Cons, then," said Margaret. "How about: *Must be stored in a plastic container during sporting events.*" She whispered the words as she wrote them.

"Margaret?" said River.

"Shhh!" said Margaret. "And how about: *Considered standard equipment for every president of the United States, so far . . .*" She looked perplexed. "But would that go under *pro* or *con*?"

"Margles? Listen up. You're either born with one of those or you're not—and you weren't. Nobody wants to think about the pros and cons of having one of those pups. Let me give you some advice: Give it up!"

"Okay," said Margaret a little sadly. "If you say so. I guess I'll just have to stick with bees."

The bus stopped at a stop sign. Margaret slowly tore her paper in half, then tore the halves in half. "Well, I'm sorry!" said River. "But that's the way it is."

Margaret shoved the torn pieces of paper into her pack. She tugged on the zipper, but it was stuck. "Stay in there," she muttered to the papers. She stuffed them farther in.

River heard a squeak. She glanced down at Margaret's pack. Inside, she could see a few dried orange peels, a rubber baby porcupine—was it a bath toy? A hairbrush, a plastic magic wand with stars floating inside . . .

What else was lurking in that clutter?

The driver clicked and ground through a long series of gears and rumbled down the highway. The bus passed a field full of hay bales standing around like sheep. A mile or so later, it approached a meadow near a wooded hillside. The kids on the bus grew very quiet.

There it was! The spotted fawn!

The fawn had appeared in the field a few weeks earlier; some mornings the kids on the bus could see it hanging out with the cows. Today it was licking the face of a black-and-white calf.

The fawn looked up at the bus, its ears alert. It sprang into the cover of the trees.

"Do you think one day it will moo?" asked Margaret.

"I hope not," said River.

"Do you think it will hook up with a cow when it grows up?"

River shrugged. "You never know."

"River?" asked Margaret gently.

"What?"

"I have a question about something."

Uh-oh. Not again!

"Do *porcupines*?" asked Margaret mysteriously.

"Do porcupines what, Margaret?"

Margaret slowly turned and gave River a look.

"Oh," said River. "I suppose so."

Margaret made a face. "Well, how do you think they manage? With all those spines? I mean I just can't picture it!"

"Margaret!" cried River, and the bus driver glanced into the rearview mirror. "Then don't try to picture it!" River whispered fiercely.

"Sorry," whispered Margaret. "I was just wondering."

"You're always just wondering," whispered River. "Put your question into Furley's confidential question box, Margaret. Instead of asking me everything."

"But everybody would know the question was mine!"

True enough, thought River. Who else besides Margaret Rothrock would want to know about the sex life of a porcupine?

"No, they wouldn't," she told Margaret. "They wouldn't suspect you because they know you aspire to be Her Royal Excellency of Bee Plumbing."

"Don't make fun of me!" snapped Margaret. "Look what you picked for a report: Bill the Wood Grub. What kind of a choice is that?"

River sat in stony silence, frowning slightly and staring absolutely straight ahead. This was the only method of Margaret Control that ever worked, and she knew now that she should have initiated it the minute Margaret had sat down beside her.

"Do you want a Pez?" asked Margaret as an apologetic gesture. She fumbled in the bottom of her pack and pulled out a small package of Pez refills. She opened the wrapping and offered the neat line of candies to River.

River took three pinks and a yellow out of the middle.

"Sorry, Riv," said Margaret.

"It's okay," said River. She crunched up the candies one at a time.

"I have so many more questions than anybody else," said Margaret. "And nobody to answer them at home. My cousin Helen camps on our couch quite a bit—and she's almost twenty. But I don't feel that close to Helen. She's kind of a flake."

River reached over and helped herself to several more candies without asking. There was going to be no fighting Margaret this morning. It was just going to be a matter of putting up with the girl, and for this River needed the kind of energy generated by Pez loading.

"To tell you the truth," said Margaret, "sometimes I feel like that deer back there. The cows put up with it. Just like you and Jules put up with me. I'm different from you and Jules. And I'm immature."

"That's not true," River lied.

"Yes, I am," said Margaret in an unsteady voice. "And maybe it's lucky—because I don't know *what* I'm going to do when I start my . . ." She looked at River. "You know." She brushed away a tear. "I've been feeling really emotional," she whispered. "I'm afraid I might have PMS."

Say something, River told herself. "Well, Furley says girls have breast buds, underarm hair and a patch—you know where—before they start. Do you really feel that you meet those criteria?"

"How many in a patch?" wondered Margaret out loud. "Would five be a patch? Or just a sprig?"

"A *sprig*?"

"Or would a patch be, say, five thousand?" asked Margaret.

"Five *thousand*?" said River. "Well, I wouldn't know. Even my pregnant mom doesn't have five thousand."

"Oh," said Margaret. "I've never seen a naked mom. Let alone a pregnant one."

Margaret had never seen a naked mom. River could hardly stand to think it.

On River's mom, the patch was currently visible as a decorative triangular rug under a generous belly with an outie belly button on the outside and a fat baby boy on the inside, probably sucking his thumb inside a pouch of water—the way he was in the sonogram image.

Aha! River could sketch a mom for Margaret!

Why not? River opened her pack and rooted through it. She found a small spiral sketchbook, with a Wint-O-Green Life Saver stuck to the cover.

On a blank page, she began to sketch a pregnant mom, naked from head to toe. "The boobs get bigger," River explained. She sketched and shaded them.

"And the belly button pops out at some point," said River.

She drew it.

"How far out?"

"I dunno. A couple of inches—no, an inch I guess. Or half-inch. Oh, and on my mom there's a thin brown line that goes south from her belly button."

She sketched it.

"Why?"

"Don't know."

River gave Margaret the picture.

"Sign it!" said Margaret. "You're going to be a famous artist someday. I've got quite a good collection of your work. And I have to tell you: This is my first nude figure drawing. Sign and date it."

River wrote *River* in the bottom right-hand corner of the picture. She wrote the date underneath. Margaret held it close to her chest and examined it surreptitiously. Then she rolled it up and stuck it into her pack. "I'll keep it for the rest of my life."

What a sweet thing to say!

"Margaret?" said River. "I'll tell you something else: Porcupines *must* have figured out a way to navigate those quills by now. Or else there wouldn't be any teeny-weeny baby porcupines. Right?"

"Right," said Margaret.

River folded her hands and looked down at them. A world without any little baby porcupines: She could have cried just thinking about it. Maybe *she* was the one with PMS!

Or maybe River could have cried just thinking about a world where there could be a little baby like Margaret who had to grow up without the opportunity of having a buck-naked mom with a sizable gut and an outie belly button roaming around the bathroom without remembering to lock the door.

River couldn't even imagine life without her mom.

Or without her dad. Or Megan. Or even without her new little tiny baby brother who wasn't even born yet; she already loved him.

River threaded her arm through Margaret's.

"You know what, Riv?" Margaret said after a moment. "I don't know what I'd do without you. The only thing my dad has ever told me about the birds and the bees is that little baby armadillos are born looking exactly like teensy-weensy versions of adult armadillos. They just climb on out, I guess. And start eating ants. Isn't that sweet?"

"Umm-hmm." Yes, it was sweet. But did armadillos really eat ants? Nobody needed to know.

Say nothing, River told herself.

Her thoughts drifted once again to the possibility of hooking up Margaret's father with Mrs. Furley. Margaret's dad was a good guy; he had a good job. According to Margaret, he had been taking weekend cooking classes in California cuisine, so he was quite capable of making a romantic dinner. And maybe even putting a few roses on the table, and candles. And reaching across the table and covering a woman's hand with his hand, and gazing deeply into her eyes.

And if the woman across the table happened to be Mrs. Furley, and they ended up getting married, everything would be just ducky for Margaret. There might even be an occasional inadvertent display of female nakedness, should Margaret happen to walk into the bathroom when Mrs. Furley was having a bath, with her shoulders poking out of the bubbles and Margaret's rubber porcupine floating against her cleavage . . .

But still. Wouldn't Margaret be very disappointed if Furley and her dad *didn't* like each other? Margaret wanted a stepmom so badly, she might really take it hard if it didn't work out.

This was a risk River might not be willing to run. Megan probably was right. River should stay out of it; if Margaret wanted to plan the impossible scheme of having her dad fall in love with somebody, then let Margaret do it herself.

However, there couldn't possibly be any harm in a little visualization, since it didn't work anyway. So why not go for it?

River closed her eyes and pictured herself crouched on a cloud, with drizzly pink and yellow sunlight all around her. She saw herself as having feathered wings like Cupid—but she would be wearing more than what Cupid normally wears, say a Peter Pan–type outfit, minus the cap, with a quiver on her back and a bow in her hand. She would reach for an arrow with a heart on the end, take aim and draw back the string—

Margaret gripped River's arm. "Wait a minute!"

"What!"

"Are baby porcupines born with quills?"

"I don't know," said River. "Why?"

Margaret made a pained expression. "Never mind," she said quietly.

They sat without speaking.

"I'm glad I'm not a pregnant porcupine," said Margaret after a while.

"I'm glad you're not a pregnant porcupine too," said River.

Eight

MARGARET'S PACK WAS HANGING from her shoulder at an odd angle as she stepped out of the bus and onto the sidewalk in front of Franklin School. Stella and Kirstin came barreling up, and Kirstin bumped into Margaret from behind.

River heard a squeak by her feet.

"You dropped this," Kirstin said to Margaret in an uncharacteristic gesture of friendliness. Kirstin held the porcupine out on the palm of her hand. Then she clamped her fingers down and squeezed the porcupine a few times. It made a few small, muffled, pitiful squeaks.

Margaret lunged at her.

Kirstin threw it over Margaret's head to Stella, and they continued throwing the porcupine back and forth, with Margaret participating in an involuntary game of Monkey in the Middle.

River watched Margaret grow more and more frantic.

Say something! River told herself. You're just going to stand there and watch while they harass your friend? What's wrong with you?

At that moment, Kirstin turned and flung the porcupine far away, and it bounced and landed by the flagpole on the lawn. Margaret rushed over to get it.

River walked toward the classroom, looking at her shoes. Why couldn't Kirstin and Stella just leave Margaret alone? But also: Why couldn't Margaret leave *them* alone? This whole war was escalating—and it was Margaret's fault too. Margaret had a history of challenging and riling up the regular girls; it had begun in preschool. Why couldn't she just accept that she'd never be one of them and move on?

Like River had.

River was cut from different cloth: from artist's cloth. She understood the Kirstins and Stellas of the world; she had never longed to be one of them. But she didn't need to confront them either. They peacefully coexisted.

At least they had so far.

River pretended not to notice Kirstin and Stella huddled together by a bush near the breezeway, giggling and pointing at something on a piece of rolled paper. She went into the classroom and began unloading her pack. She stacked a few books on her desk and—oops!—her Human Interaction notebook slid onto the floor.

DB was just passing by. He picked it up. "Look at that signature," he said. "Nobody could forge a signature like that." He stared at the *Rivers* on her notebook. "What's this? A daisy?"

River held her breath.

"You drew this?"

River nodded.

"Awesome."

Had he seen the *River & DB* in the heart in the center of the flower? She hoped not. DB flopped the notebook onto her desk.

Or maybe she hoped he had seen it!

"Still can't come to All-Stars practice?" DB asked her. "Everybody's going to Bud's after for ice cream."

"I wish," said River. Her heart thumped. "But I really can't. But I *will* be at the powwow."

"Rad."

The bell rang. Kirstin, Stella and a couple of other limo groupers came giggling into the room. What on earth was so funny?

As soon as everyone was seated, the attendance taker took attendance. Random giggles broke out around the room among the limo invitees. What was going on? River felt uncomfortable, as if they were laughing at her.

The hot lunch counter counted the hot lunch orders and paper-clipped the total to the attendance folder. In a few minutes, River the courier would deliver it to Mrs. Bagley in the office. This job thing seemed stupider by the minute. Why couldn't just one person take care of all these things—like Mr. Elmo, for example?

At least Elmo had already written the schedule for the day on the board. "As you can see, we have a slight schedule change," he announced. "Mrs. Hansen and I are doing a Sex Ed switcheroo. The Honorable Mrs. Furley has agreed to come to us today and to Mrs. Hansen's class tomorrow—"

Say it isn't true, thought River. Furley. Two days in a row?

"—so Mrs. Hansen can represent Franklin School at a meeting tomorrow morning at the district office. Flexibility, folks," said Mr. Elmo. "And team playing. It's the name of the game."

Switcheroo and *name of the game* . . . add 'em to the list, River instructed herself.

The office intercom dinged. "Yes?" said Mr. Elmo.

"You've made note of the schedule change," said Mrs. Bagley.

"That Mrs. Furley is coming to me this morning instead to Hansen? Roger," said Mr. Elmo.

"Okay, then."

"Over and out," said Mr. Elmo.

Over and out. The list was going to be endless!

Elmo began talking to the class about a current event he'd clipped out of the paper, but nobody cared about meteor showers and craters on the moon or whatever it was he was yakking about. "I can see that you are all overcome with fascination about this topic," he said, "and so are speechless. What time did everybody hit the sack last night?"

The morning slipped by. Unbelievably, River came close to tears two times between math and recess. You do *not* have PMS, she reassured herself. The fact that pill bugs were helplessly trapped in the classroom's terrarium actually was a very sad thing.

Wasn't it?

At 11:15 on the nose, Mrs. Furley arrived. And she didn't waste time getting down to the nitty-gritty. "As you went over your notes," she began, "did any of you wonder *why* testicles are located in a sac rather than being positioned up inside of the body, where they would be better protected?"

River would have been the last to admit wondering about this. So she sat without speaking, like the rest of the kids in the class. And doodled a little more on the cover of her notebook.

"Jockstraps. Cunningly devised by humankind," said Mrs. Furley, "because a delicate and vulnerable part of the male reproductive system has been left open to injury by nature. Evolutionary oversight? *I think not.* So why, why, why are such important organs hanging outside in a sac, rather than being up inside the body the way they are on a female?"

The entire class was silent.

"No ideas at all? What's the matter with you guys this morning? Margaret? I haven't heard a word from you."

"I'm thinking," said Margaret. "Can't you see my eyebrows all crunched up?"

"Yes. You do look puzzled, Margaret."

"I look puzzled because I *am* puzzled! You lost me back there. I had *no idea* women had testicles up inside the body."

Kirstin groaned.

"That's because women don't, Margaret," said Mrs. Furley. "What I was referring to in women were ovaries. And the rest of the female setup."

"Oh."

"Sorry. Anyway!" Mrs. Furley looked cheerily around the room. "It's a fascinating reason. Fascinating! The answer is this: The male reproductive cells—called . . . ?"

Don't make eye contact with her, River told herself.

"Anybody?"

Just look down at your notebook, River told herself.

"Nobody wants to say it?"

No! Was she kidding?

Mrs. Furley drew a picture of what looked like an enormous pollywog on the board. She made a sweeping gesture as though she were introducing it. "What are these critters called?"

Tadpoles, thought River.

"You know this—every last one of you knows this. Sperm!" said Mrs. Furley. She wrote *SPERM* on the board. "And so here's the answer to our question: Sperm, produced in the testicles, must be allowed to mature at a lower temperature than the rest of the body. The testicles, housed within the scrotum, hang a distance from the body, and so are cooler." Mrs. Furley stood smiling at the class for a moment. "It's just breezier down there!"

River blinked.

I did *not* just hear the woman say that, she told herself.

"Pop quiz!" said Mrs. Furley. "I warned you! Who's paper passer?" She glanced at the job list. "DB?"

DB passed out the unlabeled diagrams of the male reproductive system cautiously, averting his eyes as he put the papers facedown on everybody's desk.

Mrs. Furley wrote two bonus questions on the board: *#1. What is* preseminal fluid? *#2. What is the function of the* prostate gland?

Huh? River wouldn't be getting any bonuses on *this* quiz. She quickly filled in the blanks on the diagram, sure of every label except for one small unidentified doohickey.

She glanced around the room to see who else was finished, noting that Kirstin was busily copying the answers from Stella, who was referring to a cheat sheet on her lap.

Mrs. Furley, of course, was oblivious to this. She was sitting with her back to the class in Mr. Elmo's swivel chair, thinking, with all five fingertips of one hand gently bouncing against all five fingertips of the other.

What frightful lesson was she plotting in her head?

After a few minutes Mrs. Furley stood up and walked up and down the rows of students, collecting the papers. She took a moment to glance through them. "Henry?"

"What?"

"Get with the eraser. Those, we put in an omelette." She tapped on the bottom of the diagram. "What is their *appropriate scientific name*?"

Henry erased and rewrote the answer while she stood over him, watching. She collected his paper and straightened the pile.

"Mrs. Furley?"

"Yes, Margaret?"

"I've been thinking . . . When we were in the primary grades, we had room mothers in our classrooms—that brought us cupcakes with sprinkles."

"And?"

"And apparently," said Margaret, "the consensus here at Franklin is that sixth-graders have outgrown the need for room mothers. Which in itself is a sexist notion: Why not room *fathers*? Men can't be responsible for things related to the care of children?"

Hmmm. Where are we going here? wondered River.

"But oddly," said Margaret, "and a bit inconsistently, the sixth-grade teachers don't feel that we've outgrown the need for the extremely inane and babyish job list approach to classroom chores."

What *in the world* is she trying to get at? thought River.

"Neither do they feel that we've outgrown the need to collect behavior points to gain a reward—such as going to the Community Center."

"Let's get a move on, Margaret—I've got a lesson plan," said Mrs. Furley.

"Even though we're old enough to know that acting responsibly in the world is its own reward," continued Margaret. "So what I'm wondering is: If we're still such big babies, why can't we have the benefit of a room parent in Human Interaction class?"

"In *this* class?"

"Yes."

"Well, what would the room parent do?" inquired Mrs. Furley. "Bring cupcakes with sprinkles?"

"Ohyeah!" roared Henry. "Cupcakes!"

"Right before lunch?"

"No," said Margaret. "Bring something more age-appropriate: appetizers."

"That's a good idea," said Noah. "I get so starved during Sex Ed class I can barely concentrate."

"Like," said Kirstin, "now what are they talking about?"

"What Margaret's talking about," Noah told her, "are hors d'oeuvres."

Margaret turned and made bug eyes at Kirstin. "Ever heard of such a thing, Little Miss Limo Snacker?"

I get it! River cried out to herself. Margaret: the New Age Cupid Warrior! River could have jumped up and hugged her.

"In *any event,* I nominate my dad for room father," Margaret loudly announced. "Despite the fact that *certain people* in this room don't acknowledge that men cook." She dogged Kirstin briefly. "If elected, my dad promises napkins, paper cups with bubbly water and lemon slices floating in them and a selection of appetizers—including garlic rounds lightly brushed with olive oil and topped with fresh mozzarella and a tomato slice."

"He's agreed to this?" said Mrs. Furley.

The intercom dinged.

"Yes?" said Mrs. Furley. She looked up at the speaker above the board.

"I *second* the nomination!" said Noah in a loud voice.

"Well, good for you, girly-boy!" Kirstin called to him. "His sister plays baseball better than he does," she loudly whispered to Stella.

"Is Mr. Elmo there?" said Mrs. Bagley over the intercom.

"No, he isn't. Try the faculty room!" Mrs. Furley called up to the speaker.

Margaret stood up and walked over to Kirstin's desk and looked down at the top of Kirstin's head.

"Protecting your geeky boyfriend?" said Kirstin without looking up.

"Or no!" said Mrs. Furley to the speaker. "Actually, I think he went off campus—to Duplication Services, I think he said. He didn't sign out?" Mrs. Furley stared at the speaker, waiting for an answer.

"No," said Margaret. "I'm telling you and your brainless trendoid loser sidekick Stella to keep your fat traps shut. This is an election we're having here."

"Whoa!" whispered Henry from the back of the room.

"And your part is crooked," said Margaret. "Or is this the *Sassy* look? The 'I'm just a little baby girl who can't part my hair straight' look?" she whined in baby talk.

"I can't help it if you're like, a *total arfer*," said Kirstin.

"Never mind," said Mrs. Bagley over the intercom. "Here he is. Sorry for the interruption."

Mrs. Furley turned to face the class. "*That* was embarrassing." She held her lips very tightly together. "I expect this class to be completely quiet when the office calls."

The class grew completely quiet.

"So I think I'll take the liberty of doing *this*." With a great flourish, Mrs. Furley picked up a felt eraser and erased one point from the class behavior score. "Margaret? Please be seated. Kirstin? What's going on? Do we need to talk about this after class?"

Margaret slowly walked back to her desk.

"Well, *do* we?" said Mrs. Furley.

"*What*ever," said Kirstin.

With one swoop, Mrs. Furley eliminated another point. "Apparently, we do," she said.

"Uh? Moving *right along* here," said Noah. "Like I was saying, I second the nomination of Margaret's father for room parent. All in favor?"

"Aye!" said many quiet voices.

"Opposed?"

"Nay!" shouted the limo group.

"Ayes have it," said Noah. He walked to the blackboard. "May I?" he said to Mrs. Furley, picking up an erasable marker and uncapping it. She nodded. *Room Father,* he wrote, *Jim Rothrock.*

"Of course my dad'll want to meet with you," Margaret told Mrs. Furley. "To help plan the menu."

Yes, of course, thought River. She smiled to herself. And she knew exactly when and where this meeting should happen.

Don't do it! Megan's voice warned River.

Do it! It's now or never! River told herself.

"Mrs. Furley?" she said suddenly. "You say you're going to the powwow?"

"Yes, River. I did say that—that I would try, anyway."

"Then why not meet with Margaret's dad and talk about appetizers there?" River asked her. "Since Margaret and her dad are also going."

"My dad has a cooking class on Saturday afternoon!" said Margaret.

River looked deeply into Margaret's eyes. "But he's *skipping* it, isn't he?" she said quietly, prompting her.

"Y-Y-Y-es," Margaret said, slowly nodding.

ESP! It was working!

"He *did* say he's skipping class this week," said Margaret. "To go to the powwow. It's coming back to me now."

Keep looking into my eyes, Margaret, thought River. Stay with me here . . . "You and your dad are meeting me and my sister, remember? At the fountain. Just before one o'clock."

Margaret slowly nodded. She turned to Mrs. Furley. "So we'll see you there?"

"I don't see why not," said Mrs. Furley.

Yes! thought River.

Margaret addressed the class: "Mrs. Furley and my dad will need some idea of what we like. How many people like pâté on Bremner Wafers?"

Two kids raised their hands.

"Thai chicken grilled on skewers with peanut sauce?"

"E-e-e-e-y-a-a-a-h!" roared Henry. "Thai chicken! All r-i-i-i-ight!"

Many raised their hands.

"Prawns sautéed in garlic butter and lemon?"

"Ohyeah!" said DB.

"How about hot Brie melted inside of a gouged-out circular French bread?"

"Margaret?" said Mrs. Furley. "I have a lesson plan!"

Nine

AT LUNCHTIME Mr. Elmo detained Jules.

Again!

"Do you realize how far your group is lagging behind the other guidebook groups?" River heard him ask.

"It's all going to come together at the end," Jules told him.

Go, Jules!

"Besides, we work best under pressure," she added.

What a crock! River told herself.

Mr. Elmo pushed his glasses down the bridge of his nose and looked at her. "We do!" she cried. River hurried out of the classroom, figuring it was safer to wait in the breezeway.

Mrs. Furley, Margaret and Kirstin were talking nearby. "So stop squabbling!" Mrs. Furley was saying. "I'm sick of it and if it continues I'm calling your parents."

"*What*ever," said Kirstin. She was standing with her arms folded on her chest and her head slightly tipped to one side. She was looking at Mrs. Furley with a bored expression.

"What's with this *what*ever stuff, Kirstin?" said Mrs. Furley. "It's your new favorite word? I find it disrespectful."

"Well, you have my dad's numbers," said Margaret. She turned and made facial threats at Kirstin. "In case we *do* keep squabbling!"

River smiled to herself. Go, Margaret!

Margaret's face brightened. "Or you can talk to him about us at the powwow," she suggested, "before you go over the menu."

"I'm not absolutely committed to the powwow as yet, Margaret."

Margaret's face fell. "Then do you want his pager number again?" she asked.

"No! Just behave yourselves."

"Are we through here?" said Kirstin.

"We're through, for the moment. *After* you write a note of apology to Noah," Mrs. Furley told her. "I heard you berating him. He should play baseball better than his sister? How sexist can you get!"

"Fine. I'll apologize."

"*In* writing," said Mrs. Furley.

"Yes! I get it! Can I go now?" said Kirstin. She didn't wait for an answer; she just ran her fingers through the top of her hair, tucked one side behind her ear and stalked back into the classroom.

"I'll wait right here until that note is written," Mrs. Furley called after her.

"Recently Kirstin called me Monkey Arms," Margaret said.

"Yes, I'm sure she did. After the *long* list of names you've probably called *her* over the past several days," said Mrs. Furley. "I can't tell you two how sick and tired I am of all of this! And as I said, I have every intention of notifying your parents if it continues."

"Well. It probably *will* continue," Margaret told her.

Mrs. Furley said nothing.

"My advice? Learn to use a pager," Margaret said crisply. "Are you a technophobe?"

"Yes! And so are you! So scram!"

Margaret booked it back into the classroom.

River wandered over to the drinking fountain and took a sip. Then she casually peered through the bank of windows into the classroom. Mr. Elmo was still lobbying Jules—probably making one last-ditch effort to convince her to get the group to drop the citation booklet idea.

Ha, thought River. No chance of that.

She smiled, then frowned. For some reason, Kirstin was now standing by River's desk, using River's notebook to lean on as she wrote her apology to Noah. River watched Kirstin turn her back as Margaret passed by, to shield what she was writing.

Why didn't Kirstin use her own desk! River hated how freely Kirstin moved in and out of everybody else's space—and she was going to tell her so.

One of these days.

But for now, she *supposed* it was okay if Little Miss Queenly leaned on River's Human Interaction notebook.

As long as she didn't look too closely at the heart in the center of the daisy!

Margaret reappeared in the doorway. She stood there, Winnie-the-Pooh lunch box in hand, staring at Mrs. Furley. "You *didn't* have to raise your voice," she said.

Mrs. Furley walked closer. She put her arm around Margaret's shoulder and gave her a squeeze. "Sorry, but sometimes you really do drive me crazy, Margaret."

"You and me both," muttered Kirstin, slipping past Margaret and Mrs. Furley.

"Hey, Riv," Kirstin called. "Since you're class courier . . ."

But I'm off-duty, you jerk, thought River. It's lunch-time!

"Give this *written apology* to Noah from me, would ya?" Kirstin said, in a voice loud enough for Mrs. Furley to hear. She put a beautiful, small, sealed envelope made of thin paper into River's hand and hurried off to find her friends.

"Okay," said River quietly.

You're a wimp! River scolded herself. She should have told Kirstin to give it to Noah herself.

But what awesome stationery! thought River. She was surprised Kirstin would be willing to use such fancy stationery on a note of apology to Noah. It was like parchment paper—practically see-through. And printed on the back was a small bouquet of roses with a blue ribbon tied in a bow that twirled from the stems.

River slid the envelope into her back pocket. She wondered what heartfelt message of apology Kirstin had scribbled out in the thirty seconds it had taken her to write it.

"It's unprofessional to raise your voice," Margaret was saying to Mrs. Furley. "Even to me."

"I said sorry," said Mrs. Furley. She gave Margaret

another squeeze. "You're quite my pal," said Mrs. Furley. "And lucky you, to have such a cooperative dad. He must be quite the chef!"

"He is. And when he gets back from El Paso with new cowboy boots, he'll look like the Marlboro man. But he doesn't smoke!" added Margaret quickly. "So if you meet him at the powwow, don't worry about him blowing smoke in your face."

"No, I won't worry," said Mrs. Furley. "So, then. What have you got in that Pooh pail of yours?"

"I haven't looked yet."

"Any chips?"

"Possibly."

They began to stroll away, with River casually sauntering behind them. "What kind of an answer is 'possibly'?" said Mrs. Furley. "I have a craving for chips. Help me out here."

Margaret stopped and flipped open her lunch box. A package of chips was right on top. "Mesquite flavor," said Margaret.

"No plains?"

"Nope."

"Ask your dad to pack you plains," said Mrs. Furley. "Or sour cream and onion. I can't accept mesquite. They taste like the smell of motor oil."

"Okay," said Margaret. "But my cousin Helen packed this particular lunch for me. She's staying with me until my dad gets home. Late tonight. Mrs. Furley?"

"What?"

"You're not engaged, are you?"

"Not at the moment. Why?"

"Just wondering," said Margaret. She stretched one hand behind her back and flashed a thumbs-up sign at River.

Their voices trailed off as they headed down the breezeway together. Good old Mrs. Furley, thought River. It was nice of her to take such an interest in Margaret. And answer Margaret's unbelievably nosy questions. And give her hugs.

Come on! How long were Elmo and Jules going to blab, anyway? River griped to herself.

Finally! Jules appeared in the doorway. "Mr. Elmo keeps trying to talk me out of the citation booklets," she said to River in a very, very loud voice. Jules leaned back into the classroom. "Fat chance!"

The girls rushed away.

After eating lunch, River and Jules moved to a grassy spot behind the backstop, where they could survey the baseball game that would soon star Henry, DB and a few other boys—and Noah's sister, Lesly, who was an All-Stars pitcher on Henry and DB's team.

Lesly was standing with her arms crossed on her chest and her mitt under her arm—scowling. Apparently some pregame dirt-gathering behavior was in progress: DB and Henry had flopped down onto the ground by home plate and were grappling with DB's cap.

"Jules! Riv!" called a voice from across the field. Noah was approaching fast, waving a piece of paper. He stopped and shaded his eyes to look at Henry and DB. He stood for a moment with his hands on his hips, shaking his head. "*What* are they doing now?" he called to Lesly, who shrugged.

River wasn't sure either, but their behavior seemed to

be reminiscent of the goat fiasco on the Discovery Channel.

Noah talked to River and Jules as he approached. "While *you've* been out here watching the jocks take dust baths, *I've* been busy in the library taking Furley's Internet advice. Suddenly I'm Margaret's research assistant."

"Where *is* Margaret?" said River.

"She's been temporarily incapacitated. Listen to this—"

"What do you mean, 'temporarily incapacitated'?" River asked him.

"She's in the office! She got in trouble for throwing milk on Kirstin."

Noah covered his mouth with his hand and laughed into it, in an exaggerated way.

Good for Margaret!

River, Jules and Noah all did high fives.

"Now listen," Noah said. He gazed from River to Jules, making eye contact to be sure they were paying attention.

" 'We start with a bee colony consisting of workers and a queen,' " he read from the paper he was holding.

" 'The queen can lay eggs, which produce workers. The workers are underdeveloped females which are incapable of egg production.' "

"Stay with me, girls," Noah said. "This gets better." He briefly lifted his eyes skyward. "Or worse!" He looked back down at the paper.

" 'Workers gather nectar from flowers and concentrate it into honey, which is stored in cells in the hive.' Blah. Blah. You know this. But keep listening: 'The cells are made of beeswax, which is also produced by workers. Some cells are used to store honey and others are used to produce bees from eggs laid in the cells by the queen.' *Comprende* so far?"

"Go on," said Jules.

" 'To produce a queen, an egg is laid in a specially constructed large cell and is fed royal jelly. This produces a new, unfertilized queen. She lays eggs in cells. Her eggs develop into males, called drones.

" 'This unfertilized queen goes on a mating flight, followed by drones. Higher and higher she flies, and the highest-flying drones mate with her.'

"Now get this," said Noah. " 'Their genitals are torn away in this process.' "

Noah crossed his legs and bent his knees, then stood back up again.

" 'And the drones fall, dead, to the ground.' "

He looked from one girl to the next. "Get ready."

"Read!" cried Jules.

" 'The queen, now fertilized, returns to the hive trailing their genitals behind her.' " He grimaced.

"Yeah?" said Jules. "Then what?"

"Then nothing. That's not enough? To summarize," said Noah, "the eggs that this lady lays produce workers, rather than drones—and the colony builds back up again. The colony can divide and produce more colonies as described above. Blah. Blah. The End."

"Brother," said River.

"So! My advice to guy bees," said Noah, "is: Fly low, boys. See ya," he said, and walked away. He turned around and called to his sister: "You go, girl!"

"Wait!" cried River. "I almost forgot!" She reached into her back pocket and slid out the envelope Kirstin had given her. She ran up to Noah. "Here," she said. She gazed into his eyes and smiled. "Straight from the heart . . . from someone who *really* cares."

River batted her eyelashes at Noah. Then she turned and walked in a slinky Kirstin way back to where Jules and Lesly were watching DB and Henry in a frantic, dusty scramble over possession of a rubber base.

River didn't know whether guy goats rolled in the dirt to attract girl goats or to get rid of flies—or both. But what worked for goats was definitely working for the Deebster. He had pinned Henry to the ground and was sprawled on top of him.

River smiled to herself.

Mmmm-mmmm.

DB.

What a hottie.

After lunch it took a few minutes for everyone in the class to be present and accounted for. Noah was late for an unknown reason. He walked in and dramatically told Mr. Elmo, "Something threw me. And I needed some alone time."

This seemed a bizarre explanation for tardiness, but Mr. Elmo fully bought it. "Then come on in and sit down," he said gently.

River watched Noah walk to his seat. Just a few minutes earlier he'd been totally animated. Now he sat slumped into his chair. What was the matter with the guy?

Henry and DB came in late from the office with detention slips for failing to respond to the requests of the yard supervisor and causing the custodian to have to shinny up a pipe onto the roof of the breezeway to retrieve first base.

Margaret had been sprung from the office and was standing quietly near Mr. Elmo's desk. The report was that now her father had to come to school to discuss her recent misbehavior and the continuing conflict she was having with Kirstin, both in Human Interaction class and in the yard.

Margaret flashed River a smile as Mr. Elmo read a note from the principal, readmitting her to class and undoubtedly explaining the unfortunate lunchtime situation.

River didn't need a psych degree to figure out that Margaret had doused Kirstin with milk to ensure a meeting opportunity for Furley and Margaret's dad, in case Furley bailed on the powwow.

Ha.

River loved it!

"I'm surprised and dismayed to read this, Margaret," said Mr. Elmo. "I hope you and Kirstin can work things out." He looked past Margaret at Kirstin, who was sitting at her desk with one arm slung over the back of her chair.

"This shirt she, like, soaked with milk just so happens to be my mom's," Kirstin told him. "And it's *dry clean only*."

"You're not supposed to wear belly shirts to school," Margaret told Kirstin.

"It's not a belly shirt."

"You tied it up like a belly shirt! Like you do every other day at lunch!"

"Girls?" said Mr. Elmo. "That's enough."

Margaret cocked an eyebrow at Kirstin. "Keep your mouth shut about my Piglet Thermos and your mom's shirts will stay drier," she told her. "Although the foam rubber in that Miracle Bra *must* act something like a sponge."

Whoa! So *that* was Kirstin's secret!

"Margaret?" said Mr. Elmo in a firm voice. "Discuss brassieres elsewhere."

Kirstin lowered her eyelids and stared at Margaret until Margaret sat down at her desk. Margaret lifted the desktop, humming quietly to herself as though she didn't have a care in the world. "Take a picture, it'll last longer," she told Kirstin without looking up. She busied herself taking out a pencil, a pencil sharpener shaped like a wiener dog, a pink eraser, a small package of tissues and a solar calculator.

River caught Jules's eye. She scanned the room to see who else was being entertained by all this.

River was startled to see that Noah was looking straight at her. He mouthed the words: "We *really* need to talk."

About what?

He mouthed something else but River didn't understand. River made a puzzled face. So Noah routed a note to her, via Jules and a couple of other kids.

River opened it. *Can we talk on the phone tonight?* it said.

River looked at him and shrugged, then nodded. She wrote: *Call me. River 323–4286.* She passed it to Emily. "Back to Noah," she whispered.

Emily passed the note back, but Stella intercepted it, skimmed it, and rerouted it via Kirstin, who read it and then held it out for Noah. "Sorry!" said Kirstin. "Stella thought it was for me."

Noah quickly zipped the note into the outside pocket of his pack, which was hanging from the back of his chair.

"Okle dokle," Mr. Elmo was saying. "Let's have a productive afternoon, people. We'll begin with a little SSR. I know! I know! The schedule's a little mixed up, but let's go with the flow. Fifteen minutes of Sustained Silent Reading. Margaret? Please. Stop fooling with the plastic dachshund. No toys in class. You know the rules."

Mr. Elmo pulled the brim of his Orioles cap down over his nose and tipped back in his swivel chair.

"Right. But here we go with your standard 'No caps in class' rule violation—again!" said Margaret.

"As I have told you repeatedly, Margaret, the 'No caps in class' rule is 'No caps if you've got plenty of hair on your head to keep your head warm,' " said Mr. Elmo with his eyes closed.

"It's seventy-six degrees out!" said Margaret.

"Shhh," said Mr. Elmo. "I don't need a weather report."

Ten

RIVER REALLY HAD to hand it to Margaret. Yes, she was a nerd—certifiable, in fact. But *nobody* besides Margaret had the courage to give Kirstin Walker a spontaneous bath. Nobody!

And River would have given *anything* to have the guts to do something like that. Anything!

Nerds rule! thought River. Let's hear it for the nerds!

Which was a nerdy thing to say, even to herself.

She softly bit her bottom lip to hide a smile. "Okay, Margaret. I want to hear it all over again: *How* much milk did you throw on Kirstin when she made fun of your Thermos?"

"The whole Thermos-ful," said Margaret.

"Ha," said River. "I love it. Love it!"

"And where exactly did it land?"

"In Kirstin's face. In her hair. And all over the front of her shirt."

"Margaret?"

"What."

"I'm just so sorry I wasn't there when it happened," said River.

"Me too," said Margaret.

"You're my hero, Margles."

"And you're mine," said Margaret. The bus rumbled past the meadow. It was empty. The fawn must have been grazing or snoozing or chewing his cud with his buds on the other side of the trees.

Or her cud and her buds.

"You're sure your dad isn't going to be mad about having to come in and meet with the principal and Mrs. Furley?" River asked.

Margaret shrugged. "No, I'm not sure. And I'm worried about something else: Besides coming to school tomorrow, I've got to convince my dad to skip cooking class on Saturday to come to the powwow—and he loves that class! Plus I have to talk to him about accepting his responsibilities as room parent. And come up with a prospective appetizer menu. And miss one morning of work a week for the rest of the year."

Poor guy.

What did he do to deserve this?

"Let's talk about this room father idea," said River. "Realistically, now. How could your dad take that much time off work, once a week for—how many weeks till school's out?"

"Who knows?" said Margaret. "Let's just take this one step at a time."

Good plan.

River sat back and relaxed.

Kind of.

Something was nagging at her: Should she or shouldn't she mention to Margaret that Noah had said he was going to call her? Was it okay if she talked to somebody else's boyfriend? On the telephone? And exactly what aspect of Margaret did Noah want to discuss, anyway?

The driver slowed for River's stop. She could see Megan waiting on the corner for her. The ride was over.

I won't actually talk to Noah when he calls; I'll only listen to him, River decided, to get herself off the hook.

"Don't worry, Riv," Margaret quietly told River as River collected her things. "Even if my dad says no to missing cooking class and no to being room father, he *can't* say no to coming to school to meet with Mrs. Furley and the principal over my bad behavior."

She grinned at River.

River stood up. "See ya, Marg." She looked out the window and waved to Megan.

"Later, skater," said Margaret.

Megan flashed her mother's pink-and-black credit card at River as soon as River stepped onto the sidewalk. "Birthday present for Aunt Colleen. Victoria's Secret. Coming with me and Anton?"

"Okay," said River.

"Mom also authorized me to sign for two bras for me and two bras for you—if they have any size twenty-eight triple-A pinner."

River chose to ignore this insult.

Helene trotted along beside River and Megan as they walked up the path. Two of Helene's male kittens were in a clinch; they tumbled down the steps, pummeling each other with their back legs.

"Mom!" called River as they walked into the house. "Where are you?"

There was no answer. River set her pack down by the hat rack in the hallway. "Mom?" she called again.

"Help," said her mother in a muffled voice. "I'm having a comfort catastrophe."

River walked to the doorway of her parents' bedroom and looked in. Ever since her mom and dad had bought an egg-crate-foam mattress topper on sale for twenty-two dollars, River's mom had found it impossible to get out of bed once she got in.

Lately her mother had been creeping into bed for an afternoon nap several times a week—in fact, every day of the week. "The egg bed is calling me," she would say before waddling into her room. But it wasn't only the egg bed that was causing the problem. Six months pregnant and a gut as big as Kansas also factored into the equation.

"I have a question for you," said River.

River's mom sat up. She flipped off the bed throw and sat on the edge of the bed. With a grunt, she stood up. She crossed the room, stopping to peer at herself in the mirror. "My body has turned into pancake batter. With a basketball on the front." She turned to one side. "But I'll have you know I'm planning to enroll in an aquatic exercise class for pregnant women at the 24-Hour Club. And after the baby is born, my goal is to become a marathon runner. I may be out of shape, but there are actually *quite* a few miles left on this chassis."

"Good, Mom," said River. "Go for it. But you look fine just the way you are."

"You think?"

"Yup. You just need to tone up."

River's mother stood with her hands on her hips and stared at herself. "Is it possible to tone up knees that have completely fallen down? I could hide a key in the fold of skin above my knee! My biceps have slipped down underneath my arm instead of on top." She made a muscle for herself in the mirror. "What is your question?"

The phone rang and River picked it up from her parents' night table.

It was Margaret.

"In addition to his bee work," she began, "my brilliant research assistant, Noah, has just made an interesting discovery on the Net—"

"Oh, brother," mumbled River.

"—regarding the porcupine question."

River said nothing. She covered the receiver with the palm of her hand. "It's Margaret!" she whispered to her mom. She made a yakkety-yak sign with her fingers.

"Noah printed it out. And faxed it to me on my dad's fax machine," said Margaret. "I *love* that boy," she added with a sigh.

River thought a moment. Had Noah told Margaret he was planning to call River tonight?

Or not?

Wouldn't Margaret be mentioning this, if Noah *had* told her? And if he hadn't, *why* hadn't he? Why would Noah want to keep a conversation with River a secret?

"Porcupines!" River suddenly said. "Let's stay with the subject! I've got to get ready to go to Victoria's Secret with my sister. So hurry up."

"Okay. Porcupines," began Margaret. "According to

Grolier's, porcupines are large, spine- or quill-bearing rodents in the families Hystri-something and Erethi-something of the mammalian order Rodentia."

River yawned.

" 'The often large spines, or sharp hairs, which act as defense organs, are controlled by' "—she lowered her voice—" 'erectile muscles in the skin.' "

"Why are you whispering?" said River.

"Erectile muscles?" whispered Margaret. "You don't get it?"

"No."

"Porcupines are full of 'em," Margaret quietly told River. "They've got 'em around every single sharp hair!"

River decided to leave this topic completely alone.

"Anyway, *for* your information," continued Margaret, "the answer to our original quill mystery is—"

"*Our* original quill mystery?" said River.

Margaret ignored her. "Blah . . . blah . . . blah," she was whispering as she skimmed the paper. "Here! 'By day the crested porcupine remains in its burrow. After a gestation period of nearly four months, the female gives birth to two or three young, which initially have soft fur'! "

Margaret paused.

"And?" said River.

"And this, I would say, would be a *bit* more comfortable than spines. On the way down the chute," said Margaret.

River closed her eyes and stood there with them shut.

Margaret. Now the world's authority on erectile muscles, whatever those were.

"I've got to go," River said. "Bye."

"How's Margaret?" asked River's mom.

"Fine."

"Well, I wish you'd invite her over one of these days. I haven't seen her in a dog's age."

A dog's age?

"Anyway," continued River's mom, "to go on with my litany of woes: My eyes are beginning to fail, making it impossible for me to see the renegade hairs that are springing out of my cheeks and chin. But on the sunny side of things, I might say thank heavens I've got you and Megan to point my whiskers out to me." She leaned forward and thrust her chin out and stared at it in the mirror. "Who's got my tweezers?"

River shrugged.

"I need to shower before I go to my doctor's appointment. Dad's coming home early, so he can come with." River's mom unhooked the clip at the front of her bra, slipped out of it and then stepped out of her underwear. "Isn't he a good dad?"

Yikes!

What a gut!

"Yup," said River.

"And he told the company no more geology trips out to the desert till the baby's born."

"Good."

River couldn't help noticing how enormous her mother's rear was—it might have been the biggest, whitest thing she'd ever seen in her life. She crossed her hands in front of her face, as if to shield her eyes. "Where are my sunglasses?" she mumbled.

"River?" her mother said. "Don't you and Megan pick anything too fussy for Colleen at Victoria's Secret, okay? Colleen's always leaned more toward flannel pajamas than, say, a lace bustier . . ."

"What's a bustier?"

"One of those long, sexy, strapless bra-type tops."

"Sick," said River.

River walked out of her parents' room and knocked softly on Megan's doorjamb.

"What about a lace bustier for Aunt Colleen?" she said into the crack of the door.

"Come in here," said Megan, and River walked in.

Megan was very, *very* close to her mirror, putting on mascara. She blinked and nodded. "A lace bustier: Now yer talkin'."

"How big are Aunt Colleen's boobs?" said River.

"I forget. Call her up."

River flipped through the address book. She looked at the clock. What time was it in Chicago? Would Aunt Colleen be home from work yet? She decided to give her home number a try.

The phone rang five times; then the machine kicked in. River heard a long meow, then the tone. "Hi, it's me and Megan and we're just wondering about your cup size," said River in a cheery way. "But never mind. We're giving you a makeover for your birthday, like on *Oprah?* We need you to bring along jeans and your leather jacket—" The machine beeped and cut River off.

"Love you, bye!" she said anyway. Because she really, really *did* love Aunt Colleen. Very, very much.

But that didn't mean she had to prove it by spending practically the entire weekend with her.

Eleven

RIVER COULD HEAR Anton's car stereo coming the whole way up the street. She called shotgun and ran out the door. But the shotgun rule never applied when it came to riding in Anton's car, and Megan shoved River away from the front passenger-side door and climbed in.

River got into the backseat and buckled up. Anton looked over his shoulder at her. " 'Sup?" he said.

"Hey," said River.

Anton looked at Megan. "Hey." He reached over and touched Megan's hair.

River never would have admitted it, but her mom was totally right about the three *g*'s—especially the grunting one. And the grooming one. Anton *did* smell good; it might have been aftershave, but it could have been a heavy dose of deodorant.

They headed to the mall, with the bass turned up so far

River could feel some of the notes vibrating in her chest bone. Or breastbone.

Or whatever that place was, close to the heart.

They parked in the upper lot and walked into the mall. Anton and Megan were holding hands, with their fingers wound together. Anton's sunglasses were hanging from the front pocket of his pants.

He'd shaved his head and was bald as an egg.

River walked along staring at Anton's broad shoulders, because why not?

Nobody knew she was spying on him but her.

And there was nothing wrong with taking in a little scenery.

Megan turned and paused to wait for River and then did something unexpected: She reached out for River and put her arm around her neck, pulling her close as they walked into Victoria's Secret—the Three Pals.

Anton tried to look casual as Megan prowled through some stacks of lacy underwear and thongs on sale. "I can't believe it!" she moaned. She held up green panties with a leaf and flower print. "I just paid twenty dollars for these for Alison's birthday and now look. Three bucks."

Anton glanced at them for a second and then looked away. But there wasn't really anyplace he could safely look except the ceiling and the rug, because all around him were racks of lacy teddies; frothy, sexy nighties; and even little high-heeled shoes with fluff on them.

"Will you relax?" Megan told him.

River walked straight ahead into the bra area. She didn't have much to put into a Miracle Bra but was absolutely delighted to discover a two-for-the-price-of-one rack of glimmering satin Miracle Bras of different colors, among which were hanging some pretty tiny ones.

She looked over her shoulder and saw that Anton and Megan had gotten distracted near some robes, and that Anton seemed to be slyly eyeing some sort of black lace peekaboo body stocking hanging on one wall.

Totally eighties! Or seventies, even.

River quickly nabbed two bras from the rack: a navy and a burgundy in size 30 AA.

"Would you like a dressing room?" a very pretty old woman asked.

River followed her and the woman let her in with a key and hung the two bras on a very small hook. The door closed by itself and River locked it. She quickly pulled off her shirt, unhooked her bra and flung them onto a puffy chair trimmed with ribbon.

She put on the blue Miracle Bra.

Cleavage! River couldn't believe her eyes. What a miraculous sight! Maybe she had some Barbie-type blood coursing through her veins after all.

She got dressed again and walked out. "Shall I take those to the register?" the woman asked her.

"Yes, and now we need to find something good for my aunt," said River, handing the woman the bras.

"Like what?"

River didn't know. What would look good on an aunt, peeking out of a starched white partially unbuttoned shirt?

"I'll ask my sister," she said.

She looked across the store and

oh

my

gosh.

Kirstin's mom was here! Rooting through the sale table. She held up a ruffly lace elastic something. Gosh! What would a full-grown mom be looking at thongs for? And stringing them along her wrist, like oversized Scrunchies!

Sale fever was apparently a mom universal—no matter how much money a family had to spend. Maybe River's guidebook group should try to curtail this; maybe they should set limits on hanger banging and table tumbling.

River frowned. Good grief! How many thongs was Kirstin's mom going to buy, anyway?

River had seen a program about how you could fasten tomato plants to wooden stakes with snagged pantyhose and support ripening summer squash with discarded bras.

Maybe Kirstin's mom was going to use the thongs for gardening. Hanging lace thongs in a garden seemed exactly like something Kirstin Walker's family might do.

Maybe to scare away crows!

Yikes!

Kirstin's mom unexpectedly glanced up. River tried to duck behind a rack of two-piece PJs, but she'd already been spotted. "Hi, River! What's up?"

"Nothing," said River. "I'm just waiting for my sister."

"Oh. How do I look?" said Kirstin's mom. She put a red lace thong around her head like a sweatband.

River was speechless. What an unspeakably horrid infraction. She was thrilled it was Kirstin's mom who'd done it! Thrilled!

You should wear it like that when you pick up Kirstin at school, she thought of saying. But instead she just nodded quietly. "Mighty nice," she said.

And scurried away.

A short time later Anton, River and Megan left Victoria's Secret, with two size 34 B white cotton regular bras with underwires for Megan, one folded-up gift box and no bustier for Aunt Colleen, but instead, one cropped camisole with a snakeskin pattern, with spaghetti straps and lettuce edging, which would look awesome peeking out from underneath a shirt.

Success!

Except for the fact that River had bailed on the Miracle Bras.

When it came right down to it, there was nothing on earth Kirstin had that River wanted, including a mom who strolled around Victoria's Secret with a thong on her head.

They went straight to the food court for pizza, to celebrate. Afterward Megan called home to check in.

"Mom said Noah called for you," Megan told River after she'd hung up the phone.

"I was afraid of that. He wants to talk to me about Margaret."

"Noah's calling *you* to talk about his girlfriend?"

"I guess so."

"Don't talk to him!"

"No?" said River.

Megan scowled. "Of course not! I would kill Anton if he called up another girl to get advice about me!" She glared at Anton.

"What did *I* do?"

Megan swatted him on the shoulder. "Don't talk to other girls about me."

"Ouch! I didn't!"

Megan grabbed Anton's shirt collar with both hands

115

and hauled him close to her so her face was up against his Adam's apple. He looked down his nose at her.

River wondered: Was it true that boys had Adam's apples and girls had applesauce?

Put it in the Furley question box, she told herself.

Anton picked Megan up off the ground and carted her off over his shoulder.

I don't know these people, River told herself. She paced herself, keeping a proper distance. And hiding a small smile.

Anton and Megan were a very good pair.

It made River happy to be with them. And she happily rode home in the back of Anton's Ford, mouthing the words of the song that was playing, since nobody was looking. But she wasn't singing aloud! If she sang, Anton or Megan might suddenly turn off the radio and leave her in the lurch, singing her head off to nothing.

The phone was ringing when they got back home. "You better answer that!" her father called as River walked in the door. "It might be the phone!"

Ridiculous.

She picked up the receiver. "Hello?"

And wouldn't you know it: It was Noah. "Riv? I'm majorly confused," he told her.

"About what?"

"About what," muttered Noah, as if River were crazy. He paused. "It's like all of a sudden I'm fully somebody's boyfriend. You know Margaret—she's just so intense. It all happened so fast—I hadn't really thought about any other . . . options."

There was an awkward silence on the phone.

"I mean, it's not like I would logically be expecting any other girls to be . . . interested . . ."

River took the receiver away from her ear for a moment and held it in the air in front of Megan's face.

Megan pushed the phone away. "Just say you can't talk!" she whispered.

River listened again. "And I'm really flattered," Noah was saying, "but I don't really know what to say or think about—"

"Noah?" said River. "I have to go. Bye."

She hung up the phone.

"That was cold," said Anton.

Twelve

THE NEXT DAY, as soon as River walked into the classroom, Mr. Elmo took her aside. "As you are well aware, I don't approve of the subject matter of your group's guidebook," he began.

Yes. You *have* made that quite clear, thought River.

"But Jules informed me that you're in charge of your group's guidebook cover design, and I'm not going to let my opinion stand in the way of an opportunity for you to develop as an artist."

"Oh," said River.

"You have quite a fan club here at the school among the teachers," Mr. Elmo told her. "I'm president of it, actually." He smiled broadly and tipped forward and backward in his stadium boots. "I expect to see your name in lights someday. Or maybe under a painting in a museum."

Now what should I say? thought River.

"Thanks," she told Mr. Elmo. "I hope I won't let you down."

That was fairly dumb!

Just don't talk, River told herself.

Mr. Elmo went on to explain that the librarian had spoken with him in the faculty room during the Friday-morning coffee klatch. Mrs. Fitch had kindly offered to let River be the first one to use the new SuperGraphics software on the Mac in the library—as long as River promised to later show her how to use it.

Mrs. Bagley had then chimed in. She was at her wits' end with the student teachers! One of them had recently trapped a workbook in the brand-new, state-of-the-art copier in the office. So she made an offer too: River could use the copier in the office if she promised to tutor the student teachers on its proper use.

"I promise," said River.

"Of course you'll miss hours of classroom time today," said Mr. Elmo.

Yes! thought River. She quickly tried to make a concerned face but it was practically impossible.

Jules walked up in a huff. "Has Mr. Elmo told you the *minor detail*?" she said to River. "The whole guidebook has suddenly become due on Monday!" She pointed to the board.

Newsflash! was written there in huge letters. *Duplication Services says: No large-scale duplication available between May 6 and May 12. Machines will be down for servicing. ALL GUIDE-BOOK FINAL DRAFTS AND FINISHED COVER ART DUE NEXT MONDAY AT NOON!*

Jules glared at Mr. Elmo.

"Expect the unexpected," was all Mr. Elmo had to say

for himself. He picked up his yardstick and tapped on the schedule. *GUIDEBOOK TIME* was written in every last slot, except the last hour. "I have been as accommodating as possible, under the circumstances."

"Just get the cover done!" Jules told River. "You can finish editing the notes at the hotel tonight and get the final draft to me at the powwow."

River quickly gathered her things and left the classroom. She hadn't settled on a cover idea yet. Now her work would be complicated by the sudden availability of Super-Graphics and a copier that could enlarge and shrink stuff.

She worked at a feverish pace on the Mac in the library, including during morning recess.

During third hour, River returned briefly to class to collect signatures from everyone in her group, signed in fine-point permanent marker.

She then helped herself to Mrs. Fitch's black-and-silver marked DON'T TOUCH I MEAN IT! scissors and cut different shapes around the signatures and drew a thin black line around each edge.

Now she needed to experiment by arranging the signatures upside down on the glass of the copier and putting the paper with the background on it upside down on top of them—to incorporate all the pieces into the total cover design.

River didn't eat much lunch. She leaned over Mrs. Fitch's wastebasket and ate a few bites of her bagel and cream cheese and threw the rest out. By early afternoon she was a pro at SuperGraphics.

The layout for the guidebook cover was ready by afternoon recess, and yes, she did want and need to use the copier in the office.

She hurried across the yard; a couple of classmates stopped her and filled her in on Henry's latest escapade.

She walked into the office. Henry was sitting silently in the chair by the principal's door. She looked at him and shook her head in a disapproving way. But she was smiling inside.

What *would* the boy do next?

The bulletin board display caught River's eye because—she had never seen such a horrid mess! The flyer advertising the powwow in the park was pinned on a slant on a bright orange piece of construction paper, with a corner torn off. Below it was stapled a laminated sign that said SILENCE IS AGREEMENT. Which was totally off-center. Nearby was a terrible sign that was handwritten with red felt-tip pen on maroon paper that said WELCOME TO FRANKLIN SCHOOL.

"Hey, Riv!" said Mrs. Bagley with a smile. She lowered her voice. "My office assistant, Stella, has taken it upon herself to make a bulletin board."

"Oh," said River. So that was the explanation.

The door to the principal's office was ajar; Mrs. McPhearson was inside, chatting quietly with Margaret's father. The stage was set.

Great!

"You ready to roll?" Mrs. Bagley asked River.

"Yup." River held up an eight-and-a-half-by-eleven-inch sheet of paper with a beautiful shaded vertical rectangle on it that went from dark to light, like the sky at sunset.

"Wow," whispered Mrs. Bagley.

Inside the rectangle were silhouettes of certain objects that appeared to be flying around in space: a soccer ball, a

121

telephone, a CD player, a bottle of Coke, a plate of cookies, a baseball glove, a laundry basket. Above it, in Blades font, was written: A GUIDEBOOK FOR SIXTH-GRADE PARENTS.

"I had quite a bit of help from SuperGraphics," River told Mrs. Bagley modestly.

The best thing about the new copy machine was that it could enlarge or reduce images—perfect for what River had to do.

The worst thing about it, though, was that it was on the wall closest to the office entrance. So, of course, Stella, who had wandered in, was nosily looking over River's shoulder.

River and Mrs. Bagley experimented with River's signature, making it bigger and bigger by pressing a button with a percent sign on it and then pressing the square green Print button. And superimposing the signature on pages that already had images on them, by opening up the paper drawer and sneaking them in on top.

"Stella?" said Mrs. Bagley. "There's a sweatshirt to deliver to room six, and also, could you drop that little box by Mrs. Perkins's kindergarten room? Stanley Moss's pet fly is in there.

"And I need you to stop by the library and deliver those." Mrs. Bagley pointed to a short stack of books on a filing cabinet, with a note on top. "Mrs. Fitch is having story time. Please just tiptoe in and put the books on her desk. The note is *very* important. Set it someplace where she'll notice it—on the keyboard of the Mac. Or on the mouse pad, maybe."

"Okay," said Stella.

Stella watched as River's signature slid into the tray at

the side of the machine. "You've got the coolest signature, Riv."

Riv? What on earth would make Stella feel so friendly toward River today?

Stella picked up the sweatshirt, box and books and walked out the office door.

Mrs. Furley strolled in. "Hi, River."

"Hi."

"What's up, Henry?"

"I ate a bug," Henry told her.

"Ah," said Mrs. Furley. She paused. "Was it good?"

"It was okay," said Henry.

"Henry," whispered Mrs. Furley. She cast a furtive glance over her shoulder at River and Mrs. Bagley.

"What?"

"Did you do this to impress a girl?"

Henry shrugged.

River whistled quietly to herself, pretending to be consumed by her project.

"*Was* this girl impressed?"

Henry glanced in River's direction.

River mouthed the word *No!*

Jules would not have been impressed—just grossed out. But Jules *was* impressed with other things about Henry: in particular, his dangerous attitude, fast mouth, dark eyes and outlandish sense of humor. The fact that he was an All-Star didn't hurt much either.

"Actually, it was a grub," Henry told Mrs. Furley.

"A grub?"

Henry nodded. He looked down at his shoes.

"Now, that *is* impressive," said Mrs. Furley.

Henry smiled modestly.

"Courtship, Henry. Remember? 'All of us . . . have our own unique and mysterious ways of courting each other.' Add this to your list of things males can do to attract a mate."

"I don't have a list."

"I know you don't. And you didn't turn in a topic for your final project, either—so let me assign you one. You are to make a list of what preadolescent males do to attract the attention of girls. Begin with 'grubbing grubs.' Move on to 'throwing refreshments at each other at social gatherings' and 'infuriating wasps.' I've seen you boys out there by the trash can at lunchtime karate-kicking the yellowjackets—wow!" She softly whistled. "Now if *that* doesn't catch the eye of a sixth-grade girl, nothing will!"

She glanced at River.

River sighed very deeply and pressed Print.

"Anyway, Henry," said Mrs. Furley in her official voice, "compile a list. Interview friends and family members—"

Mrs. McPhearson waved Mrs. Furley into the office.

"Oops! Have to go," said Mrs. Furley."

She straightened her blazer. She made a serious face and turned to Mrs. Bagley. "I think grubs are staple diet items in certain cultures, but can you give Poison Control a ring?"

Mrs. Bagley frowned at Henry. "Who in his right mind would eat a grub?" She made a terrible face. Then she tipped her head back to look at the list of emergency numbers tacked to the wall by the phone. "There's ipecac syrup in the emergency medical kit if they say we need it," she mumbled to herself.

"What's ipecac syrup?" said Henry.

"Stuff that makes people hurl," said Mrs. Bagley.

River peeked through the doorway into the principal's office. Just think of it: The moment had arrived. Destiny had brought Margaret's dad and Mrs. Furley together. Random chance? Uh—we don't think so, River told herself.

"Mrs. Gladys Furley?" Mrs. McPhearson was saying. "This is James Rothrock, Margaret's dad."

Margaret was right: Her dad *was* workin' a kind of a Marlboro man look—with a yuppie touch.

"Please call me Jim," said Margaret's father to Mrs. Furley. He stood up and took Mrs. Furley's hand. "It's a pleasure to meet you."

Cool! He'd gotten a tan in Texas. But the bad news was . . . oops.

Infraction!

Margaret actually *had* let him wear the cowboy boots. He could be cited for those pups.

Mrs. McPhearson poked her head out of the doorway and looked at Henry over the top of her glasses. "I'll be with you in a few moments, young man," she told him. "Where's Margaret?" she asked Mrs. Bagley.

At that moment Stella wandered back in. "Stella?" said Mrs. Bagley.

Stella sighed and stared at her. "What?"

"Send Margaret Rothrock to the office, would you? And then you're excused to go back to class. Thank you."

Stella turned on her heel and marched back out again.

River's heart raced as she waited for Margaret. Gladys and Jim—together at last. Was it karma—or just one spontaneous, well-aimed splash of milk?

A moment later Margaret walked stoically in. "Hi,

Marg!" whispered River. She could barely contain her excitement.

Margaret didn't speak.

She sat in the chair next to Henry's. River could see that her eyes were brimming over.

"Margaret! What's wrong?"

"How *could* you?" Margaret answered in a whisper. She looked down at her hands, and two tears rolled down her cheeks.

River's heart thumped. "How could I *what*?"

Margaret closed her eyes. Her chin was trembling.

Mrs. McPhearson opened the door. "Oh, now," she said, when she saw how upset Margaret was. "Don't cry. We'll work this out."

Mrs. McPhearson put her arm around Margaret's shoulders, and Margaret covered her face with her hands and sobbed. "Margaret!" said her dad as Mrs. McPhearson gently led her into the office. "Come on now!"

"Please!" said Mrs. Furley. "This just isn't the end of the world here!"

Margaret looked back over her shoulder at River. "It is to me," she said in a trembly voice as Mrs. McPhearson closed the office door.

Thirteen

RIVER RETURNED to Mr. Elmo's class and sat quietly at her desk. She was exhausted and sick and tired of layouts and signatures and reducing and enlarging stuff. She'd have to finish the project first thing on Monday morning.

Margaret didn't show up. Apparently she'd gone home with her dad.

Jules had no idea what was going on.

And Noah wasn't talking.

River ran through the day's events in her mind. Had she said the wrong thing about Margaret to somebody? She felt a little panicky. How could she have said or done something so wrong and not even know what it was?

She felt out of touch. Maybe she shouldn't have worked so hard on the cover for the stupid guidebook.

Mr. Elmo had carefully laid out his Indian art and artifact collection on a table covered with a beautiful handwoven horse blanket. He held up a granite ax head. "Think of it," he told the class. "Hundreds and hundreds of years ago, a man held this in his two hands, attached it to a sturdy piece of wood, lashed it there with rawhide strips . . ."

Now if Margaret had been there she might have said, "How do you know this man wasn't a woman?"

But Margaret wasn't there. She'd gone off, in a huff or a flood of tears.

"Mr. Elmo, I have to go back to the office," interrupted Stella suddenly. "I forgot! Mrs. Bagley still has a bunch of stuff that needs to be delivered and she asked me to pick a helper and I want it to be Kirstin." She glanced at Kirstin. "We've got work to do," she whispered with a smirk.

Mr. Elmo opened his desk drawer and handed them each a laminated office pass. "Scram."

The students watched intently as Mr. Elmo turned the ax head in his hand, and listened as he wondered out loud who might have used it and where. And for what.

Gosh, the class was quiet without Margaret. And Kirstin and Stella.

River glanced at Noah. He was looking straight into her eyes. River's heart thumped. What was going on? He was acting like a psycho!

River tried to concentrate on the Yakima pouch with a beaded pig on the front and the Pomo basket that Mr. Elmo was showing the class. She put her head on her desk and listened to a CD of authentic powwow songs.

The bell rang. River gathered her things and walked outside. Kids said goodbye to each other and went off in different directions. "Have fun," River told Jules.

"I just wish you were coming to the All-Stars practice

with us," said Jules. "And out for pizza with me and my dad afterwards."

"Yeah," said River. "Me too."

DB and Henry walked past and waved goodbye to River. They were carrying their gym bags. DB's looked heavy—it undoubtedly held his cleats, catcher's mask, glove, chest protector, shin guards . . . Mmmm-mmm! Guys in uniforms. Too bad she wouldn't be able to check him out this afternoon, crouching behind the plate.

River lingered outside the classroom, hoping to talk to Noah as he left. He would probably know what was going on with Margaret. "Noah?" she said quietly as he came out into the breezeway. But he rushed right past her as if she weren't there.

What was going on?

River wandered toward the parking lot. Instead of riding the bus, she was waiting for her mom to pick her up so they could leave earlier for San Francisco. Suddenly Kirstin ran up. "Riv!" she huffed. "Where's Henry?"

"I don't know. Why?"

Kirstin shook a large sealed manila envelope, with the shape of something boxy inside. A great big CONFIDENTIAL had been stamped on the front with the office stamp.

"Stella was totally supposed to deliver this to Henry before school got out," Kirstin told River. Kirstin frantically looked around. "But then, like, she delegated it to me for some reason."

Thank you for sharing, thought River. Who cares!

"I can*not* believe this!" whined Kirstin. She sighed with her entire body. "Henry's mom dropped it off at the office. He *needs* it!"

"He and DB are walking to practice," River told her.

She turned and pointed toward the field. "See? They're right over there. Walking with Lesly."

Kirstin pushed the package against River's chest. "Here. Henry totally *has* to have this. In case he takes a fast ball below the belt. You're class courier. Just race over and toss it to him! Please! I'm going home with Stella on her bus and it's about to go without me!"

Kirstin raced away. She turned and shouted: "Have a great weekend! Sorry we couldn't invite you to the limo party! If anybody drops out, we will!"

River plopped her backpack on the ground. I can't believe this! she told herself. I sign up for class courier and suddenly I'm an after-school athletic supporter delivery service. This is just a *bit* beyond my job description! she grumbled to herself. She decided to carry the envelope by just one corner, to distance herself from it.

"Henry!" she shouted. But Henry didn't hear her. She could feel it sliding around in the envelope. "Henry!" she shouted again. She looked down at the package.

Yikes!

Only a flimsy paper envelope separated her fingers from Henry's jockstrap!

"Catch!" she called. She tossed Henry the package. She quickly turned and hurried back toward the parking lot, just as a big yellow bus was pulling away from the school. Kirstin and Stella were looking out the window at River, heads together, laughing.

Do *not* look back, River instructed herself. But she couldn't help it. She glanced at the boys over her shoulder. Henry had opened the envelope and was looking inside. He pulled out a note and read it. Then he slid a silver box out of the envelope and opened the lid. He reached in and pulled out something red—then threw it into the air as if it had bitten him.

It fell into the grass and Henry and DB stared at it. They looked over at Lesly. She picked it up by pinching it with two fingers. She dropped it back into the box and Henry slammed the lid back on.

They all looked in River's direction.

She quickly turned her back. She couldn't help chuckling to herself. Henry's mom had wrapped the boy's jockstrap up in pink tissue paper and put it in a silver box. *Un*believable! Now *that* was an infraction if she had ever heard of one! No wonder Henry had such an outlandish sense of humor—he'd inherited it from his mother.

River hoped her own mom would have as much fun having a son as Henry's mom apparently did. But good thing River's dad would be around—that was for sure.

River wouldn't be able to provide much support for her little brother in the athletic department. Until this very moment, she hadn't even known that a jockstrap could be red!

Fourteen

"THERE ARE THE BOYS," said River's mom as River climbed into the car. "Gosh. Everybody's getting so big. Is that *Henry* over there, staring at us?"

"Don't honk and wave!" cried River.

Her mother turned and looked at her.

"You scared me," said River. "I thought you were reaching for the horn."

"I wasn't. The horn is here," said River's mother. She patted the padding on the steering wheel below the air bag.

"Don't do that!" River cried. "You just did that to freak me out."

"No, I didn't. What's wrong with you?"

"Nothing!" said River. But something *was* wrong—really wrong. Margaret had practically been full-out sobbing in the office.

"How *could* you?" she'd asked River.

How could I *what*? thought River. But a guilty feeling crept into her belly. The situation must have involved the phone call from Noah somehow. River really should have told Margaret he'd called. And why hadn't she? River didn't even know. She'd call Margaret to straighten things out the minute she got home.

"You sure nothing's wrong?" River's mother asked her.

"Positive. I just don't want to talk."

"Fine. Are you packed?"

"Yes."

"Guess what I found in the pocket of my overnight case?" said River's mother. "A surfer troll. That goes to show you how long it's been since I spent a night away from home. I put him on your dresser."

"He isn't mine!" River cried out.

"Well, whose is he, then?"

"How would I know! Am I the only person in the family who's ever owned a surfer troll?"

"Well . . . yes."

"I'm telling you. My surfer troll is with all my other trolls in a box under my bed labeled 'Trolls'!"

In the same vicinity as a cute little card I forgot to show my ex-pal Margaret, River added to herself. With a nice little Eeyore on it, getting his tail tacked back onto his butt.

River turned her head and stared out the window. They drove past houses and a stretch of countryside. They passed the meadow near the grove. The field was empty. Even the cows were gone.

"Mom?" said River. "Speaking of surfers, can I just ask you something? Dad's a geologist. Has it *ever even occurred to him* that his daughter *might* benefit from a take-your-daughter-to-work experience of going to a geology conference about volcanoes in Hawaii?"

They turned onto River's street.

"Who's this?" said River's mom. A new black Mitsubishi Eclipse with a spoiler was parked in the driveway. River's mom pulled in beside it.

Margaret was slumped down in the passenger seat of the Eclipse. Her dad hopped out of the driver's seat and hurried over to talk to River's mom through her car window. "Sorry to pop in on you like this," he said apologetically. "It's just that Margaret's so upset and she won't say what's wrong. Only that she needs to talk to River."

"Good heavens!" said River's mom. She looked over at River. "What's going on?"

River shrugged.

"I don't know how I'll ever get through this," said Margaret's dad in a low voice.

River unlocked the door and swung it open.

"Well, they're making a guidebook for us," said River's mom. "An instructional manual of some sort, if that's any consolation." She gave him a look.

"Where can I get a copy?" Margaret's dad whispered as River got out of the car. "I'm desperate!"

River approached Margaret's side of the Eclipse. The radio was playing a sad country song. Without looking at River, Margaret flung a small parchment-colored envelope out of the car window. It landed on the lawn.

River picked it up. A little bouquet of roses was printed on the back. It was the note Kirstin had written to Noah, which River had inadvertently delivered to him, thinking it was an apology. Margaret brushed back tears. "Did you think he wouldn't tell me? My relationship with Noah is based on trust, *River*," she said in an unsteady voice. "Something that *you* wouldn't know anything about."

River lifted the flap of the envelope and pulled out the paper inside. Under a printed bouquet of roses on top of the stationery, Kirstin had written, very, *very* neatly, in handwriting resembling River's:

> *I am writing this, Noah, because*
> *I know you like Margaret but*
> *I really want to go out with you.*
> *I've liked you since forever.*
> *I've liked you since fifth grade.*
> *I wanted to ask you out before Margaret did but*
> *I was scared you'd say no.*
>
> *Love,*
> *River*

River stared at the signature. It was a perfect forgery. Perfect! What a snake Kirstin was!

"And River?" Margaret fumbled in her shirt pocket and took out a small slip of paper. She held it out the window, pinched between her thumb and finger. "Here," she said. She let the paper go. "I also found *this* in Noah's backpack. Dad!" she called. "Let's go!"

River watched the paper flutter to the ground. As she picked it up, Margaret closed the window and turned up the radio, really loud. River heard the door lock click.

Margaret leaned on the horn and her father threw up his hands and got into the car.

River looked at the slip of paper; it was the note she'd

passed to Noah with her phone number on it. She stared at it for a minute, not knowing what to say or think. "Honey?" said River's mom. "Move away from the car."

Margaret and her dad backed out of the driveway, with Margaret looking straight at the dashboard, arms folded against her chest and tears streaming down her cheeks.

"What was *that* all about?" River's mother asked.

"Nothing," said River. She walked ahead of her mother. Two of Helene's kittens were hissing at each other, backs arched and tails fully fluffed and pointing straight up.

"How can there be nothing the matter?" called River's mom.

River went into the house and sat on the edge of her bed. How long would it take Margaret to get home? A Mitsubishi Eclipse should be able to haul cheese, thought River. She waited five minutes and dialed Margaret's number. She listened to the phone ring seven times and then hung up.

There was no answer ten minutes later, so River called Jules. Maybe Jules and her mom hadn't left for the baseball practice yet. River got the answering machine. "Hi, Jules?" she recorded after the beep. "It's me, River. Call me *the minute* you get home."

River hung up.

Duh.

That was a fairly dumb message. Jules wasn't even going back to her mom's. After practice, Jules's dad was picking her up, to go for pizza and a movie.

To say nothing of the fact that River herself would be headed to San Francisco.

Get a brain! River scolded herself. And pack, you liar! You said you were packed. Her suitcase was opened up on the rug, half full. She slid the guidebook notes into the elastic pouch in the suitcase lid. She'd have to do all the final editing tonight—so she could give the final draft to Jules at the powwow. Would Margaret and her dad even go to the powwow? At this point, River doubted it.

River folded her flannel nightgown with bears playing baseball on it, and tucked it into her suitcase next to her jeans. She stared at the pattern. Were any of the boy bears wearing plastic Tupperware armor inside red jockstraps?

What time was it? Maybe if everybody hurried, she could convince her parents to stop by the baseball field on their way out of town so she could talk to Jules about Margaret.

Something on her dresser caught her eye.

Dude! thought River. I remember you! She picked up a small troll doll and smoothed his green hair. What were you doing hanging out in my mom's suitcase all by yourself? Everybody was wondering where you were!

Tears filled River's eyes. Life used to be so simple . . . She pulled the troll box out from under her bed and lifted the lid. She gently put the surfer troll in next to his friends.

See? Everything's fine, thought River. Everybody's back together.

Soon Candace would be home from Hawaii. They'd look back on this and laugh. Or better yet, Candace would help River plot revenge against Kirstin!

River went into the kitchen. "Sorry I got mad at you, Mom," she said quietly. "But you need to learn the difference between a surfer and a skateboarder."

"Okay. I will. Honey?" said her mother. "I really, really wish you would tell me what's going on with Margaret."

River pulled a quart-sized plastic bag out of the Ziploc box and hurried back into her room. She put her black flip-flops into the bag and sealed it. Rubber thongs: reminiscent of the upside-down backless ventilated underwear for crazy people from Victoria's Secret.

The phone rang and River ran out to the hall to answer it. "Hello?"

She could hear background noise, voices and cheering. "River?"

It was Jules. "*Tell me* you didn't deliver that elastic thing to Henry in an envelope after school."

"I can hardly hear you!" said River.

"That's because I'm on a pay phone right next to the snack shack. *Shut up!*" Jules snarled to a boy who was making fart noises near the receiver. "*And get away from me, you jerk!*"

"Jules?"

"Did you or didn't you?" said Jules a moment later.

"To Henry? Yes!" said River.

"*Why?*"

"*Why?*" said River. "Kirstin told me to!"

There was a pause. "*Kirstin* told you to?"

River heard a few more loud Bronx cheers.

"*I said get out of here, you total loser jerk!* Just a minute," said Jules. Then River heard in the background, "Ouch! Ow!"

It grew quiet.

"I just can't believe you would do that, River" Jules said quietly. She hung up the phone without saying good-bye.

River's heart sank. Jules was mad at her. Because Henry was embarrassed. But why was this River's fault?

The package said CONFIDENTIAL. Why did the big dope open it in front of everybody?

It was River's fault—because she should have told Kirstin to deliver the stupid thing herself!

River knocked on Megan's doorjamb. Megan was stuffing stuff into an Eddie Bauer duffel bag. "What?"

River walked in. "Packing?"

"Nope," said Megan. She crammed in a hooded sweatshirt. "I'm just sittin' here on the rug in front of a duffel bag because, well, I like to! It's fun."

River didn't smile.

"Did you pack conditioner and shampoo?" Megan asked her.

"Not yet," said River. "But I will." She sat on the edge of Megan's bed. The covers were all rumpled up and there were little pointy pieces of stale French bread crust everywhere.

"What's the matter?" said Megan.

"Oh, I don't know," River began. She stared across the room. A prickly feeling came over her. "That's a Victoria's Secret gift box," she said in a quiet voice. "Isn't it?"

"Right. It's Aunt Colleen's present."

"Please tell me that the Victoria's Secret box is not silver. With pink ribbon," said River.

"What, you don't like the color scheme?" Megan asked her.

Tears sprang into River's eyes. "Is there pink paper inside?" she asked in a wobbly voice.

"Uh. Eeeyeah," said Megan.

River covered her face with her hands.

Fifteen

RIVER BLEW HER NOSE a few times with Megan's Puffs Plus tissues with skin lotion included in every last tissue so you wouldn't chafe your nostrils.

Chafed nostrils.

Now, this had to be the least of River's problems.

She and Megan had put it together: First River had been set up by Kirstin to deliver the forged love note to Noah, to break up Noah and Margaret. Then River had been set up by both Kirstin and Stella to deliver something from Victoria's Secret to Henry—most likely a red thong—to break up Henry and Jules.

And to completely discourage DB from wanting to go out with River. Why would DB want to go out with a girl who'd given his best friend a pair of backless underpants!

And speaking of best friends: Where was Candace while all this was going on!

That frightful truant!

Candace should have been here with River, to help deal with Kirstin and Stella—not in Hawaii with her parents, feeding her face with passionfruit pie!

River finished packing and stood with her suitcase near the front door. When her father walked in, she politely stepped aside. "How's my girl?" he asked her.

"Fine."

He searched her face. "Fine? You don't seem fine."

"Well, I am!" snapped River. "Can we get going? You're late."

"I am?" Her dad checked his watch. "No, I am not."

River huffed out a fat sigh. She crossed her arms on her chest, Margaret style. She even thought of tapping one foot, the way Margaret would do.

"Honey?" called River's dad. He walked into the kitchen. "What's going on?" River heard him whisper to her mom.

"I have no idea! Jim Rothrock brought Margaret by after school and—"

"Dad? I said: Nothing's wrong!" barked River.

The house grew very quiet. "Apparently she's having problems with her friends," River's mom whispered in the kitchen. "So now she's mad at all of us."

"Ah. That makes sense," said her father.

"Shhh!"

Her dad walked back out into the hallway, smiling. "So!" he said cheerfully. "Shall we hit the bricks?"

Hit the bricks? thought River. She could hardly *hardly*

wait till she had her citation booklet. She picked up her suitcase and opened the door.

"Be careful where you step," her father warned.

Helene was nursing all five of her kittens right smack on the welcome mat. What a motley group! The kittens were kneading Helene's belly with their paws. Ick. Helene's head was turned to one side; her eyes were shut. She was purring and licking underneath her front foot so enthusiastically she was practically pulling her tongue out of her own head.

Now really. How could this behavior be natural?

One of the boy kittens looked up at River and blinked. Grow up, she thought. You big baby! Haven't you ever heard of cat food? Get up and eat for yourself, you dumb oaf. She checked Helene's food dish. Two yellowjackets were grazing at the bottom of it—probably boys.

Go out and get on some flowers! River thought to herself.

Did yellowjackets cart around flower sperm, or did only bees do that? River didn't know or care. She only wished DB were here to karate-chop their heads off or drown them in the water dish.

If he was even speaking to her at this point. Everybody else in the world seemed to be mad at her. Why not him?

River picked up her suitcase and stormed down the stairs. She got into the backseat of the car and slammed the door. She sat with her suitcase on her lap. Maybe I won't even wear my seat belt, she thought. She drummed her fingers on the top of her suitcase. Where was everybody, anyway?

She closed her eyes. How could *anybody* believe that River would give Henry a thong!

How could *anybody* believe that River would make a move on Noah? With or without Margaret in the picture!

She could try to call Margaret from the hotel. Margaret, of course, would probably hang up on her—or tell her cousin Helen to tell River she wasn't home.

River could call Noah—but Noah's number was unlisted, because his mother was a surgeon. What a snob!

River felt a little flutter of hope. Maybe she could call the Deeb! He had a level head; he could help straighten this out.

She felt a little better. She'd call DB from the Pan Pacific Hotel. If they ever got there. She leaned forward and honked the horn so her family would hurry up.

"I have to feed the cats!" called her dad from the porch.

No, you do *not,* thought River. Helene was as fat as a pig. She would be fine for one night and one day without cat food. And her five piglets had plenty of milk to guzzle. Those horrid little stinky skunks with sour milk drizzling down their chins!

River booted the back of the front seat. And left a shoe print on it. She said nothing when her family finally got into the car.

"Got your suitcase?" her mom asked her.

"No, Mom," said River. "This is a square black Labrador retriever I have here in my lap."

"I can do without the sarcasm," her mother quietly told her. She turned to River's dad and smiled. "So! Away we go, hmm?"

"Yup." River's father slowly backed out of the driveway, glancing into the rearview mirror and then looking back over his shoulder.

"Clear, Dad," Megan told him. "Dad?" she said. "I said, it's clear. You can go. There's a hair on your collar. Are you, like, shedding at all times?"

River rode the whole way to San Francisco without speaking a single word to anybody, unless it was to answer a question directly asked of her and her only, and then she answered using the absolute minimum number of words. "Well, this promises to be a real fun family event," Megan muttered as they crossed the Golden Gate Bridge.

They qualified as a carpool, so there wasn't any toll. "How 'bout them apples, huh?" said her dad as he drove on.

What apples! Something *had* to be done about this man!

The car came up to a light.

There's the Exploratorium! River almost cried out, but she caught herself in time. Nearby, she could see the statues of Greek ladies standing around on top of some pillars, with soft light glowing in the drapes of their gowns. This was the spot where she and the Deeb had once stood at the edge of the lake and fed mallard ducks Honey Nut Cheerios together, while the goddesses looked down at them from above. She began to feel a little sunnier, remembering this.

And yes. She totally would give Deeb a call this evening, after he had gotten home from the practice. "Mom?" she said quietly.

"Yes?"

"Did you bring along the phone book?"

"The phone book? No, why?"

"*Why?*"

Her mother turned around and looked at her.

"Well, what if I want to call somebody?" River said. "Do you think I have everybody's phone number memorized?"

"If you need a telephone number outside of your area code," River's father told her, "dial long distance information: 1 plus the area code plus 555 plus 1212."

River made a soft *t* sound, like this: "Tttttuh." This was to indicate that his suggestion was preposterous.

" 'Tttttuh' what?"

"Well, how am I going to remember that?" said River.

"I'll help you, Riv," said Megan, in a surprising move toward reconciliation, given the fact that she hadn't done anything wrong to begin with.

"Okay," said River.

"Whose number do you need?" Megan whispered. "Signal, Dad," she told her father.

"DB's," whispered River. "I'll call Deeb and he'll help me straighten this out."

"Ah," said Megan.

Her dad turned on the blinker, rolled down the window and fully extended his arm. "Is this good enough, Instructor?" He vigorously pointed his finger and pulled into traffic.

They drove past a park. A guy was standing on the lawn, flying a kite as big as a doghouse. Two buff women wearing white visors were running along the sidewalk. "That's going to be me as soon as the baby's born," said River's mother, to change the subject.

"But not with your ponytail poking out of the back of a visor, I hope," said Megan.

"Why not?"

"Why not!" cried Megan. "Are you serious?"

"Nobody talk," said River's mom.

River's dad drove down Bay Street and turned right on Columbus. "Dad?" said Megan. "Your hands should be in the ten o'clock and two o'clock position on the wheel, in case you're interested."

"Thank you," said her father. He gripped the steering wheel and stared straight ahead with his neck extended. "Is this correct, Instructor?" He maintained this ridiculous posture even as he pulled into Valet Parking in front of the Pan Pacific Hotel.

A guy wearing a red jacket with gold buttons opened the car door for River's mom and helped her out. He loaded River's suitcase and Megan's duffel onto a cart with a piece of rug on the bottom of it. "Careful with the Labrador retriever," River's mom told him.

"What?"

River glared at her.

"Nothing." River's mom smiled at him innocently. Then she made a quiet little *woof!* sound that only River heard.

The huge open atrium in the center of the hotel lobby was at least ten stories high. River plopped onto a huge couch in front of a golden fireplace while her dad found a house phone and called Aunt Colleen.

A crackling fire in May, River thought. Now, whose idea was this? And what would Margaret Rothrock of the Environmental Police have to say about this particular brand of wasted energy? If she were here.

Nothing, because Margaret wasn't even speaking to River.

Five minutes later, Aunt Colleen came charging out of one of the glitzy glass elevators and ran across the rug. "I can't believe it!" she cried.

River's mom picked up her shirt to display her belly. Now, *that* little maneuver was going *straight* onto the infractions list.

They hugged. Then Aunt Colleen hugged the girls. "Back to back!" she said to Megan. They stood up tall and River's dad measured the tops of their heads. He picked up Megan's fist and held it in the air.

"Aunt Colleen?" said River. "Can we go up to the room and use the phone?"

"We just got here!" said River's father.

"First things first, *Dad*," said Aunt Colleen. She slipped a plastic coded room key out of her back pocket and handed it over. "I think you'll find the accommodations acceptable," she said in a formal way.

River and Megan took the elevator up to the eleventh floor. After a frustrating episode involving the plastic card and the door handle, the girls gained entry to the suite: two bedrooms, two baths and a sitting area. River picked up the wet-bar checklist. "Want a Coke for nine dollars?" she asked Megan.

River checked out a bedroom. She paused in the dressing room. Gosh. What a great makeup area. There was a skirted stool placed under a vanity, with mirrors that could be adjusted so you could see the back of your head. If that wasn't good enough, a movable magnifying mirror with a light on it was mounted on the wall. River should sit her mom right down here with some tweezers so she could get after those renegade chin hairs!

A stack of expensive robes was sitting on a small table

near a card that politely reminded people not to steal them.

"Get in here!" called Megan. "Are you going to call? Or not?"

There was a strip of white paper across the toilet that guaranteed it was a germ-free place to sit. River put the lid down and sat, while Megan punched the significant number of buttons it took to get past the hotel operator and onto the information line for the correct area code.

River listened as Megan negotiated with the operator. After a lengthy process of elimination, she scribbled DB's number down on a notepad in a golden notepad holder, tore it off and handed it to River. "I'll call in a little while," River told her. "I don't think he'll be back from practice yet. They were going for ice cream after."

Megan sat on the skirted stool in the dressing room and retouched her lipstick. Then she sat River down and painstakingly put lipliner and lipstick on River's mouth, and a little mascara and a tiny bit of brown shadow. Next they decided to change clothes, with Megan flinging stuff everywhere and River carefully folding her things into one of the scented drawers.

River wandered back into the sitting area. She sat on the love seat and stared at the phone on the coffee table. She read the list of instructions on top of the phone. "Press eight first and wait for the dial tone," Megan told her.

But what exactly would River say if DB answered?

"Then press one, the area code and then the number."

River hadn't called DB since the fourth grade!

"Hurry up!" cried Megan. "I want to get out of here!"

"First I'm trying Margaret again." River punched the

numbers in and heard the phone ringing at the other end. "Hello?" said a voice.

"Hi. Is Margaret home?"

"Yeah—hang on." It was Helen, Margaret's older cousin.

"Margaret!" Helen called. There was a long pause. River thought she heard whispering in the background.

"Like, who *is* this?" said Helen.

"River."

"Oh," said Helen quietly. "Well, Margaret's not home."

"Okay," said River. "Thanks." She wanted to say, Yes she is! Put her on the line because I need to tell her I didn't write any stupid notes to Noah!

But instead River just said goodbye.

And immediately punched in DB's number. The phone rang twice and his mom answered. "Is DB there?" asked River.

"Who's calling, please?"

Infraction number one.

"River."

"*River?*" said DB's mom.

"Ummm-hmmm."

"River! How are you, honey?"

"Fine," said River.

Infraction number two.

"Gosh, it's great to hear your voice! DB isn't home yet."

"Okay," said River.

"He's over at Bud's with some kids." DB's mother lowered her voice. "*Just* between us girls, I ate some bad linguine with clams for lunch and got the runs!"

This, I don't need to know, thought River.

"So I had to call my neighbor—Kirstin's mom—and ask her to bring DB home for me."

Infraction number three.

"She can just drop him off here when she picks up Kirstin and Stella. I guess all the guys 'n' gals decided to go down to Bud's for ice cream."

River's eyes grew rounder. Kirstin and Stella were *with DB at Bud's?*

"You kids sure are growing up," said DB's mom.

River's heart sank.

"Shall I have him call you when he gets in? . . . River? Are you there, honey?"

"No. That's okay," said River. "Thanks," she added quietly.

"Is everything okay?"

"Mmmm-hmm," lied River. She tried to sound chipper. "Everything's fine. Really!"

"How's your sister? Megan, right? What grade's she in now?"

"She's a junior."

"Wow! Time flies."

River said nothing.

"Well, I'll tell DB you called."

"Okay," said River. "Bye." She hung up the phone. Then she tipped over sideways on the love seat and rested her face against her two hands, which she was holding together to cradle her cheek. And closed her eyes.

"What happened?" called Megan.

Two teardrops grew bigger and bigger and headed slowly downhill. One seeped through River's fingers and the other rolled down the side of her nose and into her mouth.

Great. DB and Kirstin—at Bud's together. Maybe they were sharing a milk shake with two straws. With their foreheads touching, like her mom and Dicky Dingman—like two kids in a Norman Rockwell painting. With Stella watching over them, like an angel from hell. Two more tears escaped and whizzed down the paths of the others.

"What happened, Riv?" asked Megan again.

"Oh, nothing," said River. "The Deeb is just hangin' with Kirstin at Bud's, that's all."

Megan sat on the edge of the love seat. "Oh." She patted River's shoulder. "Guys are such jerks."

"I'm not going to the powwow tomorrow," said River. "I'm tired of thinking about Jules. And DB and Henry. How could they believe I'd give Henry a thong?"

Megan shrugged.

"You'll have to give Jules my guidebook notes," River told Megan.

River barely ate at Planet Hollywood. And she hardly talked, either.

Back at the hotel, she completed the final revision of the guidebook, wrote GUIDEBOOK FOR SIXTH-GRADE PARENTS on the front of the envelope, then went to bed.

River dreamed of Kirstin and DB slow-dancing at the powwow, in the center of a circle of Aztec dancers. She woke up with her heart pounding. It was nine-thirty. Aunt Colleen and their parents had already gone to Fisherman's Wharf. Megan and River ordered room service and a woman in a uniform appeared twenty minutes later, pushing a cart with a pink tablecloth on it. Megan signed the bill with a flourish. They sat in bed and ate.

"I guess I'll go to the powwow after all," River announced.

What choice do I have? she thought. She wouldn't have let Megan ride all the way to Live Oak Park alone on the bus. What if some perv tried to sit next to her?

"Good. You can hang with Anton and me," said Megan.

"I will," River told her. "Because you know what? I'm sick of my friends. And I'm tired of dealing with Margaret. Would you like to know the latest? She's actually been scheming to hook her dad up with Mrs. Furley at the powwow today!"

"Trying to control how people feel about each other," said Megan. "What a waste of energy."

"Yeah," said River, as if she would never even consider being part of such a ridiculous plot.

"Like that psycho brat Kirstin," said Megan. "Did she really believe she could break up Margaret and what's-his-name?"

"Noah."

"With some stupid forged note? Or that she can break up those other two with a red thong?"

"Henry and Jules."

"Didn't it occur to Kirstin that you guys would figure out what she was up to?" asked Megan. "Doesn't she know true friends work stuff out?"

"I guess not," said River.

River drew a bath and luxuriated in the tub, piling suds on her chest in conical shapes and wondering how long it was going to take for her to develop a sizable set of the real things. She heard the door click. She heard

Megan ask, "Did you guys have fun at Fisherman's Wharf?"

"Yup," Aunt Colleen answered.

"Where are Mom and Dad?"

"Oh. They've gone back to the room. I said we'd stop by and say goodbye before I walk you to the bus."

"Riv!" called Megan. "I'm giving Aunt Colleen her present!"

"Go for it!" River called. She wasn't feeling very festive. But she added happily, "Happy birthday, Aunt Colleen! Open up your present! I'll be right out!"

She heard the rustling of tissue paper. "It's the bomb," she heard Aunt Colleen say a moment later.

Good. Aunt Colleen liked the camisole. But that was no excuse for her to say "It's the bomb." And if River hadn't completely finished editing the guidebook notes last night, she would have added it to the list.

She pinched her nose and dipped her head under the water to rinse her hair. Then she sat back up in the tub and looked down at her chest. Grow! she told herself.

By the time River got out of the bath and got dressed, the birthday aunt had been completely transformed. Her hair was pulled off her face and balled up in the back and was clamped by one of Megan's plastic clips with teeth on it. Some wisps of hair in front had accidentally-on-purpose been left out, and they fell around her face in a sexy way. She was wearing jeans, black boots and a white shirt—as per the phone order. The camisole peeked out, revealing a bit of cleavage. Megan was doing Aunt Colleen's lips in deep, dark wineish-maroonish-brownish lipstick.

"You look like a movie star!" River told her.

"I hope not Gene Hackman," said Aunt Colleen.

153

River decided to give Margaret one more chance to be reasonable.

She dialed the number from the bathroom. "Hello?" said Helen.

"Tell Margaret: I did *not* write *anynotetoanybody*," River quickly said. *"Somebodyforgedmyname!"*

"Huh?"

"Please tell Margaret that River *didn't write any notes* and River *needs to talk to her.*"

"Like, who *is* this?" said Helen.

Duh.

"It's River," said River.

"Oh." Helen paused. "Hmmmm."

River waited.

"Well, I guess, like I told you last night, Margaret's not home."

Oh sure. "Could you give her the message when she *does* come home?" said River.

"I'll see what I can do," said Helen. "But Margaret's hardly talking to me either," she added. "For some reason she's holding me and her dad responsible for whatever it is that's going on between all you guys at school—"

"Oh," said River.

"—and apart from figuring out you're in a fight we don't even have a clue what's coming down! We're completely in the dark here!"

If River stayed on the line even a minute longer she was in danger of Helen wheedling out classified information.

"Oh," River said. "Well—bye."

She hung up. Margaret was punishing her family for no reason? Cool! Maybe Margaret *was* growing up after all.

Sixteen

RIVER AND MEGAN GOT off the bus, and there was Anton, leaning his fine self against the bus hut. River tucked the guidebook revision under her arm and they all headed toward the powwow. Ahead she could see booths set up in a circle around the edge of a grassy field.

A man with long hairy legs wearing short cutoffs walked briskly by. As soon as he passed, Megan froze. She held both of her hands in the stop position and rocked a little bit, with her eyes shut, as if she were trying to get her bearings. She popped her eyes open.

And River had to agree. There should be an age limit set on guys wearing Daisy Dukes in public, there really should.

Megan softly elbowed River as a handsome teenage Fancy Dancer walked past, his chest naked and smooth under a breastplate made of bones.

"Eeeyup!" whispered River under her breath. She glanced at the dancer's beautiful beaded cuffs, heard the ringing of the bells fastened above his gorgeous beaded moccasins.

This boy was mighty fine.

Megan paid for Anton and River, and they walked into the park. What a spectacular day for the dances! The sky was China blue; the clouds were high and feathery. Poplar leaves stirred in the wind. The air was damp and fresh; it smelled of campfire smoke. Just ahead River could see Margaret standing near the fountain with her dad.

River's heart thumped. She walked in another direction.

But Margaret ran right over. "Riv!" she squeaked.

River folded her arms on her chest and stared at Margaret. "What?"

Margaret walked very, very close to River and said in a low voice, "I don't know *how* I could have ever believed you wrote that love note to Noah. And Noah's so embarrassed that he believed it, I think he's afraid to show up. But Riv? As an apology, Noah *did* take quite a bit of time to get to the bottom of all of this." Margaret pressed her hand against her chest. "Don't you just *love* him?"

Margaret took the guidebook envelope from River and put a folded paper into River's hand. "Check this out," she said. "It's a copy of the note that went along with that underwear you delivered to Henry with no butt in it."

River looked down at the note.

"The way this all came down is that Lesly got suspicious when Henry opened the package you gave him," said Margaret. "She was standing right there and saw the thong."

"Shhh!" said River.

"So, after Bud's, Lesly extracted the note from Henry

that was in the package with the red thong. She showed it to Noah as soon as she got home. I guess Noah had told her about the love note Noah thought you sent *him,* and—"

"Shhhh!"

"Anyway, after a lengthy investigation that involved *many* phone calls, Noah faxed this to me around noon. Isn't Noah *fabulous*? Did you know he's considering working for the CIA when he grows up?"

"No!" said River. "Stop talking!" She read to herself,

> Henry,
> Hit a home run for me.
> I really want to get with
> you over the summer—after
> schools out. I really don't like
> DB like everybody thinks.
> I like you but I dont
> want Jules to find out.
> Keep this for
> good luck and think of me.
> You are the steamiest stud!
>
> Love, River

"The way Noah figured out you didn't write it," Margaret told River, "is that it's missing two apostrophes! Isn't he *brilliant*?"

"*That* was the hidden clue?" asked River. "The *steamiest stud* part didn't catch Noah's eye?" River gave the note back to Margaret. She looked over at Megan and Anton, who were discreetly pretending not to be listening. "We'll catch up with you guys in a little while," she called to them. "I'll hang out with Margaret. Her dad's right over there."

"Check in with us at two o'clock by the lemonade stand. And don't leave the park," Megan told her.

Gosh. Megan had just turned into River's mom!

Anton and Megan strolled away. Anton looked back over his shoulder at River. "Later," he called.

"Later, skater!" called Margaret, and River cringed.

Then Margaret slyly spoke behind her hand. "I want you to know that something good came out of all of this. My dad got so worried about me, he didn't say one thing about having to cancel cooking class. He even brought a cookbook along!"

"Really?"

"Yup. Mrs. Furley called last night and agreed to meet us here today, even though she had 'other plans.' "

Margaret shuddered with excitement and let out a little squeal. She tightly squeezed River's arm. "Here she comes!"

River turned to see Mrs. Furley walking in their direction. Mrs. Furley was wearing glasses with small, oval gold frames. Her hair was fluffy around her face; no barrettes. There was even sunlight winking in her curls! "Hello, girls!" she called to River and Margaret.

They waved.

"Hi, Jim."

Jim Rothrock smiled.

Margaret marched closer and gave her dad the guidebook envelope. "Hold this for us, okay, Dad? It's our final guidebook revision—check it out. If you see Jules, give it to her. We'll be looking at the Apache shawls."

Margaret turned to Mrs. Furley. "We'll just let you two

figure that menu out by yourselves," she said, clasping her hands in front of her chest for a moment.

Then she whirled around and dragged River away by her arm.

"Gosh, Margaret—be a little more obvious!" River told her.

They stopped at the first booth they came to. Margaret pretended to be looking at some buttons made of antler. "What are my dad and Mrs. Furley doing?" she asked in a low voice.

River glanced over Margaret's shoulder. "Laughing," she said.

"What now?" Margaret asked ten seconds later.

"Talking."

"About *what*?"

"How would I know!"

"Keep watching!" said Margaret.

Oops. *Now* what was going on? Oh my gosh! A good-looking, middle-aged man with salt-and-pepper hair had walked over and joined them!

No! River cried out to herself. *Say it isn't true!* She watched as Mr. Pepperhair picked up Mrs. Furley's hand and patted it.

"Now what?" said Margaret.

"I hate to tell you, *but* . . . I think Mrs. Furley already has a boyfriend," said River quietly.

"Oh," said Margaret. She slowly turned around. She gazed in her dad's direction for a long moment. "I guess it wasn't in the stars then," she said in a sad way.

"I'm sorry, Margaret," said River.

"Me too," said Margaret.

And River really was very, very sorry. Here was Margaret, this perfectly fine little girl, all ready to grow up—with not even a big sister to look after her at a powwow.

Only a dad.

And only a dad would be available to buy Margaret maxipads with adhesive strips and Velcro tabs—when she finally needed them.

River could just see it now: Margaret's dad, looking bewildered in a sea of pads at Payless: overnights, thins, slims, winged, tabbed, maxis, minis, pantyliners . . . Margaret's dad, sitting in a puffy, upholstered flowered chair outside the dressing room at Victoria's Secret. Embarrassed to tears, probably.

Darn that Mrs. Furball!

Well, River and Megan could adopt Margaret as a sister. They could invite her shopping every once in a while, if Margaret promised never to say "Later, skater."

They could even snag a supply of pads for Margaret if River's mom happened to come along; River's mom was an excellent pad and tampon wrangler. River didn't mind sharing her mom.

Margaret and River strolled from booth to booth with arms linked. Neither talked much.

"I'm thirsty," Margaret said.

"Well, let's get you a lemonade, then," said River in a big-sisterly way. They stood in line and bought one gigantic lemonade in a paper cup. They sat on a hay bale and shared it, waiting for the dancing to begin.

"Do you really think Henry believed I wrote that note? And gave him that thong?" River asked.

Margaret stared into the lemonade as she drank from it. "At first he did."

"Do you think Henry showed it to Jules?"

"Nope." Margaret took another long slurp and passed the cup to River. "Boys don't do stuff like that. The Boy Code doesn't allow it. They keep information to themselves."

"Well, I know Jules at least knew about the thong! She hung up on me about it!"

"Well, somebody else must have told her about it. News like that travels fast."

Margaret paused.

"To tell you the truth, River, Noah didn't show me that love note you supposedly gave him. I ran across it in his backpack—along with your phone number. Stella and Kirstin told me it was there."

River took a drink. " 'Ran across it'? 'In his *backpack*'?" She looked sideways at Margaret.

"I know, I know! It was wrong for me to snoop," Margaret admitted. They passed the lemonade back and forth.

River heard a commotion behind them. "What the heck's the matter with a guy in a pair of shorts?" said a familiar voice. It was her dad's! River turned to see her mom and aunt laughing uproariously.

"What are *you* doing here?" said River.

"Oh—the minute Aunt Colleen got back from putting you two birds on the bus these two goofballs realized: What the heck," said River's father. "They'd rather hang out with you guys at the dances than clatter through the city on a cable car. Or poke around in the Exploratorium. I would have been the last to disagree, after that frightful omelette at the Wharf."

"Cool!" said River. She jumped up and threw her arms

around Aunt Colleen. What a disaster! she thought as she gave her aunt a long squeeze. All these grownies hanging around the powwow and spying on the kids!

"Besides," said River's mom. "We were a little worried about you, River. *And* Margaret." She looked at Margaret. "Everything okay?"

"We're fine!" River told her in a very firm voice. "You worry about *everything*." She introduced Margaret to Aunt Colleen.

"Where's Megan?" said River's dad.

"With Anton."

"Ah," he said. "Well, if you see them before I do, tell them I'd like to barbecue for everyone this evening. Aunt Colleen checked out of her hotel and is camping on our couch tonight; we'll be taking her to the Airport Express first thing in the morning."

"Great!" said River. But for now, how would she ditch these three?

River loved her family deeply—really she did. But that didn't mean she had to spend a whole powwow with them! Let them get lost and sit on the grass together and share a taco—and let her mother drop it all over the front of her gut.

Why not? The powwow was a celebration of life. How better for a pregnant mom to celebrate life than with her husband and her sister on her sister's birthday with spiced ground beef and garlic, refried beans, diced tomatoes, lettuce, grated cheese, chopped onions and hot sauce on fry bread?

"Margaret and I were just going to walk around for a few minutes," River began. "Where shall we meet you guys in, say, half an hour?"

"Is your dad here, Margles?" said River's mom.

"Yup." Margaret pointed across the grass to the fountain.

"You think you and your dad would like to join us for a barbecue later on? At our house?"

"Yup."

River could see that Mrs. Furley and her boyfriend were just now walking off together. Margaret's dad was watching them go, with his cookbook and the guidebook notes in his hand.

River's mom waved. "Yo! Jim!"

Yo?

My mother did not just shout "Yo," River tried to tell herself.

"These girls!" called River's mom. "Huh?"

Infraction!

River's mom and dad and Aunt Colleen walked toward Jim Rothrock. "One minute they're at war; the next minute they're friends," called River's mom. "This parenting. It's a roller coaster!"

"But help is on the way!" called Margaret's dad, holding up the clasp envelope. "I've got an advance copy of the guidebook rules!"

River thought of following her parents for a few steps so she could police the conversation. Instead, she and Margaret watched at a distance as her mom introduced Aunt Colleen, and Aunt Colleen and Margaret's dad shook hands. "Gosh. Your aunt is pretty," whispered Margaret.

They moved closer to eavesdrop. "Brother," Margaret's dad was saying. "I guess I made it through the storm, but now I've been railroaded into being room father for anatomy class—or whatever it is."

"Human Interaction," said River's mom.

"Yes, I guess that's what it is." Margaret's dad looked into Aunt Colleen's eyes. "Anyway, I just finished talking to Margaret's teacher, Mrs. Furley. She's requesting prawns sautéed in garlic and lemon for twenty-eight kids. . . ."

Aunt Colleen was looking at Margaret's dad's mouth as he was talking. They still hadn't let go of each other's hands. Was anybody besides River noticing all this?

Margaret gently put her hand on River's arm.

Yes.

Someone else was noticing.

"It's cosmic," whispered Margaret. "I swear it!"

The drummers started drumming, and River could hear them beginning to sing in high, faraway voices.

"Hey," said someone behind River. It was Deeb! He helped himself to River's lemonade cup and took a drink.

"Where's Henry?" River asked him. DB nodded in the direction of the food stands.

"Is Jules with him?"

"Yup. So's Noah. Noah's explaining about Kirstin, Stella, thongs, notes, drawings and jockstraps. So I left."

Margaret began hopping up and down on her tiptoes and waving. "Noah!" she called. "Wait up!" She raced away.

In the background River heard a horn blasting. A white stretch limo had pulled up to one side of the park. Arms and hands poked out of the sunroof. Kirstin and Stella stood up and began making *Wooo! Wooo! Wooo!* noises by patting their mouths and yelling at the same time. What a horrid racist thing to do!

I do not know these people, River assured herself.

She turned and called to her parents. "We'll be around!"

"Hey, Deeb!" called River's father. "What's up?"

"Hey!"

That was enough conversation. River nudged DB to get going.

A minute later Kirstin and Stella were right behind River and DB, laughing. They had snuck past the ticket collector to gather ticket stubs that had fallen into the grass. "What up?" Kirstin called to River and DB.

Neither answered.

"You have to admit it's not very brainy to, like, duh! totally leave copies of your signature in the recycling box," Stella called to River.

"Or scribble your signature all over your notebook where, like, *anyone* can trace it?" called Kirstin.

"No, no, no-o-o-oo-o!" Stella said in a playful voice. "I wouldn't do that again!" She smirked at DB. "How did Henry like the fab present from River?"

DB said nothing.

"And, Deeb—how did you like the drawing River tucked into your gym bag?"

"I didn't," said DB.

"River *thought* you'd totally dig a self-portrait, but . . . oh *well*!" said Stella. She burst out laughing.

What self-portrait? thought River.

"Hey, dude!" Kirstin shouted to the handsome dancer with the breastplate, beaded cuffs and bells. "Like, strike a pose!" Kirstin moved her disposable camera up close to her eye. The dancer turned his back.

Suddenly River grabbed Kirstin's wrist. "Ouch! Let go of me!" cried Kirstin. "Ouch! Are you *crazy*?"

"You're not supposed to take pictures of the dancers," River told her. She wrenched the camera out of Kirstin's hand. She walked over and threw it into the fountain.

"I totally cannot believe you did that!" cried Stella.

Actually, neither can I! thought River.

The camera bobbed to the surface of the water and began circling round and round, with two huge bronze goldfish spitting on it. Kirstin looked at the camera with her mouth open and both hands on her head.

"What is *with* her?" Stella yelled. "Is she, like, *losing it*? That camera cost my mother eleven bucks!"

"Totally *all* of my party snack shots are on it!" cried Kirstin. "I can't believe you!" she shrieked at River.

I can't believe me either, thought River.

"Uh, what *are* you?" shouted Stella. "Like, Little Miss PMS or something?"

River had to admit, PMS was a possibility. Maybe this *was* her first formal premenstrual attack. And if it was, then so be it. If an empty egg sac pumping out grouchy little hormone messengers provided the extra motivating force for River to toss Kirstin's camera into the drink, then maybe ovulating at age twelve had a useful purpose after all.

River and DB watched Kirstin scramble up onto the stone ledge that circled the fountain. "I have twenty-two party pix on that roll!" she shouted.

Balancing on her knees, Kirstin leaned way, way over the water and tried to coax the camera to shore. "Come here!" she whined at the camera. "Right now!"

Stella scrambled up beside her. Both girls began pawing at the water, to try to draw the camera closer. And

River couldn't help wondering: What was goin' on with the matching leatherette miniskirts?

River and DB strolled away. "By the way," said DB. "I never believed you put this in my gym bag. . . ." He reached into his pocket and handed River a folded note. "Don't open it up *here,* though," he warned her. He took a large swallow of lemonade and looked sideways at River.

Now what! River lifted one corner of the note and peeked in.

She could see part of a larger drawing: one bare leg. Below the toes, just above River's signature and the date, squeezed in—in handwriting similar to River's—were the words: "Dear DB, I love you and I want to have your baby."

River slapped it closed. It was the pregnant mom drawing she had given to Margaret! How did Kirstin and Stella get ahold of it? Those terrible weasels!

"Wait here!" River told DB. She shoved the folded drawing into her back pocket. She circled back to the fountain and—oops! She accidentally bumped the back of Kirstin's miniskirt with her shoulder, and—uh-oh!

She also accidentally shoved Stella off balance.

Too bad!

They both flopped into the fountain. But . . . oh *well*!

"Buh-bye!" River said, giving them both a few generous splashes of water in the face for good measure before disappearing into the crowd with DB.

You did it! she cried out to herself.

DB handed her the lemonade. "You're cool, River."

In the distance, River could see a guy in a tux standing beside the open back door of the limo. Soon Kirstin and Stella, looking like two drowned rats, climbed in.

River took a little sip of the lemonade. She looked down at the floating ice cubes and lemon slices and smiled a wicked little smile. She stood beside DB, without talking, in a group of people who had gathered to watch the Flag Ceremony begin.

River could feel the fingertips of her left hand softly brush the fingertips of DB's right hand. He gently wove the tips of his fingers between her fingers, then slid his fingers down between her fingers. And oh my gosh! Without even planning it, they were holding hands.

Four Native American men were assembling at the edge of the circle. Three of them carried flags: an American flag, a POW/MIA flag and a California Republic flag. The fourth man held the Eagle Staff. Soon they would walk solemnly into the grassy dance arena. Across the field, River spotted Mr. Elmo. In anticipation of the Flag Ceremony, he was already standing at attention, with his Orioles cap over his heart. What a grand old Elmo Bird he was!

What would Elmo say when he found out about the bird bath the Limo Princesses took in the fountain? What would Jules and Henry say?

And Margaret? And Noah! *And Candace,* when she came home from Hawaii!

Best yet, what would Megan and Anton say? River could hardly wait to tell them!

If the powwow was going to be the same as last year's, after the Flag Ceremony, the Grand Entry and the Sneak-up Dance, the man with a microphone would invite everyone at the powwow to join in a Friendship Dance.

The head man dancer and the head woman dancer would begin the line; others would join, and the line would

168

grow longer and longer. Eventually the people would form a huge circle, moving to the rhythm of the drums.

River's mom and dad would break the guidebook rules; they'd join the dance. So would Mrs. Furley and Mr. Pepperhair . . . and Aunt Colleen and Margaret's dad . . .

Gosh. Aunt Colleen and Margaret's dad! They'd be together tonight at the barbecue.

For all River knew, she and Margaret were destined to be cousins!

After a while, the head man dancer and the head woman dancer would break out of the circle and lead the line so that it doubled back on itself. Everyone would find themselves face-to-face, shaking hands and looking into each other's eyes.

Underneath their feet, the bulbs of naked lady flowers would be stirring—when the time was right, they'd send up shoots of leafless stems and bloom together in the park. Bees would crawl into their pink cups and take off again, their thighs loaded with pollen.

Above them clouds would drift.

River's baby brother would be born. A boy!

River just loved boys.

She looked sideways at DB. His head was high. His jaw was set. His eyebrows were low because he was squinting. Something had caught his attention—he followed it with his eyes, like a mountain lion studying its prey. River could see his temples moving. She studied his profile.

Mmmmm-mmmm. What a mouth.

Without looking down, DB fished an ice cube out of River's lemonade cup with his fingers.

And bounced it off the brim of Henry's baseball cap.

ABOUT THE AUTHOR

Mavis Jukes is the author of *Expecting the Unexpected,* available from Yearling Books, as well as a number of books published by Knopf, including the Newbery Honor Book *Like Jake and Me, Blackberries in the Dark,* and *It's a Girl Thing.* She lives in California with her husband, an artist, and is the mother of two daughters.